BOOKS BY JAY CRONLEY

Cheap
Shot

Cheap Shot

by

Jay Cronley

Atheneum · New York · 1984

Library of Congress Cataloging in Publication Data

Cronley, Jay.
  Cheap shot.

  I. Title.
PS3553.R544C5   1984   813'.54   83-45499
ISBN O-689-11445-1

Published simultaneously in Canada by McClelland and Stewart Ltd.
Composition by Maryland Linotype Composition Company,
Baltimore, Maryland
Printed and bound by Fairfield Graphics, Fairfield, Pennsylvania
Designed by Mary Ahern
First Edition

*Inspiration for this novel was provided by
my daughter's auto insurance agent.*

Cheap Shot

One

Trout looked out his window at the dark offices and wondered, as they waited for a red light to change, if there was any truth to the rumor that there was no way they could screw this up.

He had heard that often enough, and it was starting to get on his nerves and make the back of his neck tight.

"Our pulse rate won't even go up," Finch, who was driving and smiling, said. "I give you my word on it."

One of the reasons Trout was uncomfortable was because he had no experience with perfection. Another reason was that the truck he was riding in was the size of a steamboat, but didn't corner quite as well.

"Make a left when the light changes," Trout said.

"That's why I'm signaling, Trout, exactly the way I did twenty years ago when I made a ninety-eight on the driver's test. They took two points off because I honked too much."

Finch made the left turn, missing a car parked at the near

curb by two feet, and a car parked at the far curb by three feet, and he moved the truck cautiously along a one-way street, which was deserted.

Thank God, Trout thought; and he was immediately sorry he had thought that. He had enough on his mind without bringing religion into the picture. On the one hand, he would sincerely appreciate some blind luck or divine intervention. But he didn't think God would go out of His way to help a person take approximately thirty million dollars' worth of stuff that didn't belong to him. That the truck was rolling smoothly along probably meant there was no God, which was depressing.

The question of whether or not there was a God, or whether or not Trout wanted Him eavesdropping, was not a healthy topic for debate in the front seat of a potential getaway truck; so Trout concentrated instead on a subject with a much simpler predicate.

They were on their way to a museum to relocate twenty or thirty million dollars' worth of assorted masterpieces—the difference depending on the hour and whether somebody pulled a muscle during the loading and had to take a few minutes off.

They were going to put the treasure from the museum into a truck they had rented, and they were going to transport the masterpieces to a safe place, a house in the Connecticut countryside. From there, they would make a deal with the curator or board of directors or whomever and arrange for a few million dollars to be transferred to a bank near, or preferably even under, an alp.

Once the busy work was done, the museum could have its previously priceless artwork back as good as new, and probably even better, seeing as how it could have been lost forever.

Insurance would cover the ransom, the three or four or five million. Trout had visited the morgues of several newspapers, and he had learned that a pay-back request of between ten and twenty-five percent was reasonable in situations like this. He was distressed to read, however, that most of the people who had tried to relocate and then resell artwork worth millions wound up with fifteen years instead of fifteen percent.

That not so much as a pot of ivy had been taken from the museum in question in the last three or four decades was incidental, at least in the opinions of Trout's partners; for he had thought of a way to get around the fact that the museum was protected by one of the most sophisticated security systems in the world, and the fact that guards lived inside it at all times.

Trout had come up with a way to neutralize all the wires and laser beams and pit adders or whatever else might be up there protecting the works of art.

Before they made their move on the museum, they were going to swing by this one precinct house and steal the police. That way, there wouldn't be anybody to come and get them when the alarms went off.

"It's going to be like kids playing in a sandbox," Finch said, making a right turn without so much as nicking anything. "A sandbox full of gold dust."

Trout rolled his window down and leaned outside and reported back that the end of the truck had missed a fire hydrant by no more than nine inches and a parking meter by no more than six inches.

"We could have always hired some winos and used ten or twelve Toyotas instead of this thing," Finch said, maneuvering the van into the middle of another one-way street.

The next turn wouldn't loom menacingly on the horizon for a little bit, so Trout sat back and closed his eyes and tried to relax.

It was hard to believe this wasn't still practice.

When Trout first presented his idea to three of his most overdue friends, two of them were so impressed, they quit their jobs on the spot. They used Trout's telephone and called in their resignations and were ready to get on with it that night. They didn't have particularly stimulating jobs, though. One of them was in the nostalgia business. He wore a signboard advertising a diner and walked around Lincoln Center from ten in the morning until three in the afternoon. The other made threatening telephone calls for a bookie. The third person in Trout's apartment the night he mentioned his idea for becoming uncontrollably wealthy slept on it and quit her job the next morning.

And she was earning twenty-eight thousand dollars as a beautician.

Trout wasn't particularly comfortable with that kind of pressure.

But from the very beginning his friends had encouraged him to hurry the hell up and set the whole thing to music. Because nobody had ever thought of stealing the police to keep from being caught, Trout's associates were of the opinion that there could be no adequate defense. They begged him to quit wasting time with nonsense like research and street maps.

They had always been impatient when the chips were down and the last card was being dealt.

They had all become acquainted a couple of years before at Hangar 10-Z where approximately four dozen people had gathered to bid on 1,465 pieces of unclaimed luggage that had been sitting around an average of six months.

After half a year or so, each airline sells all the bags and baskets and trunks and briefcases that passengers either lose or forget or don't want.

Most of the people at the big auction were representatives of companies that take the brass locks or leather handles or suede linings from the luggage and convert the leftovers into something else, like furniture. It was ironic, then, that as the bidding got serious four of the finalists were individuals representing only themselves.

When the bidding passed the $4.50-per-bag-or-box-or-whatever mark, only five competitors remained; and since nobody had ever offered that much for a piece of unclaimed luggage, the auctioneer called a five-minute recess, and some cold beers were passed around to break the tension. During that pause the four individuals, called together by Trout, compared notes and learned that they were about out of money. So they formed a quick partnership and went head to head with a man named Shimmerhorn who represented a company that recycled cardboard.

Trout's group won the 1,465 pieces of unclaimed luggage for a bid of $6.38 per bag, which added up to $9,346.70, plus operating expenses. After they paid a mover $335 to haul the stuff to a warehouse that rented for $850 a month, their investment was roughly $11,000.

It was like a treasure hunt at first. They'd pick a bag and rip it open and dig for gold and rubies and cameras and radios and leather jackets and jeweled gowns and perhaps even a million dollars' worth of something illegal that once belonged to a smuggler subsequently killed in a shoot-out.

They opened suitcases for two weeks and five days.

They opened suitcases until their fingers started swelling.

The highlights were:

One pair of new cowboy boots, size 14.

A leather coat that was unfortunately excessively padded and looked as if it had been filled with air. The leather was also cheap and cracked.

A Minolta camera without a switch that rolled the film forward.

A Bulova watch.

A billfold made of snake-skin.

A sawed-off shotgun.

They also found a lot of cheap clothing, including 425 pairs of pajamas, which aren't worth much used. They sold a mountain of bad clothing for eleven cents a pound.

After they added up their losses, which came to around fourteen hundred dollars apiece, Trout did some undercover work and learned that the man who had been bidding against them was an airline employee whose goal had been to run the price up.

Trout also learned that while buying unclaimed luggage was basically a decent gamble, working in the hangars where it was stored was pure genius.

Trout guessed that his group was about the fifth set of people to see what was inside the luggage, the first being the people who transported the unclaimed material to the hangar, the fourth being the people who swept up.

That, the act of breaking into lost bags, was why people performed seemingly dreary jobs at airports; and it was also why some of them drove Jaguars.

Although Trout and his new friends got taken to the cleaners (they had to have everything washed and dried before they could even sell it by the pound), they promised to stay in touch and have a drink every couple of months in case somebody came up with something better than investing in old pajama futures. Trout even had a couple of dates with the female member of the bag-buying syndicate, but they were too poor to have much fun.

None of them really took the others all that seriously until Trout suggested dabbling in some art. He came up with the plan one afternoon when somebody broke into his apartment and stole his Mr. Coffee machine. He went to the nearest police station and reported the crime and was laughed at.

There might as well not *be* any police, Trout decided on the way home.

And here he was, seeing to it.

"You're going the wrong way on a one-way street," Trout

said, recalling all the times when he had cautioned his associates against overconfidence.

Obviously, these warnings hadn't been taken to heart.

"So?" Finch said. "*Let* somebody stop us. We'll throw him in the back. Besides, this street is quicker."

Trout thought briefly about jumping out of the truck.

But then, maybe they were right about his idea.

Finch stopped the truck in front of the Thirty-third Precinct four minutes ahead of schedule, which gave Trout the time he needed to polish the signals.

Trout was very thorough.

He got out of the truck and walked around to the driver's window and made a cutting motion across his throat. "That means stop."

Finch looked at Trout's neck and nodded.

It was drizzly and foggy, and there was nobody on the street.

After Finch memorized the stopping signal, he looked at his watch. It was seven minutes after eleven. He wouldn't be doing any backing until exactly ten after, so that left a full three minutes for more discussion of the signals, which had been pretty easy to grasp when they had first begun going over them four months ago.

"And this," Finch said, pointing to his left, "means move it left."

"That's *your* left," Trout said.

"It's your left, too, Trout. You're going to be standing on the sidewalk facing the same way I am. It's going to be *all* our lefts."

"What if you look in the side-view mirror?"

"Then your left is going to be my right."

"That's what I was worried about," Trout said, frowning.

Finch told him that he worried too much. Some of it was normal, since they were, in fact, pointed the wrong way on a

9

one-way street in front of a police station. But it wasn't as if they had been out cruising and drinking beer and had decided on the spur of the moment to steal some hubcaps. Finch had practiced backing the van up against some steps a dozen times, and he had never once hurt anybody. He assured Trout that he would handle the potential problem with the signals by not looking into the side-view mirror.

"I'll hang my head outside and look back at you, person to person."

"That's fine," Trout said.

"Listen, Trout, you need to relax and let nature take over. This is going to go perfect."

"I just don't want you backing over anything."

"Like what?" Finch asked, looking around.

"Me," Trout said.

He turned and walked to the steps leading up to the Thirty-third Precinct and gave Finch the first signal, which was very elementary. He wiggled his fingers, exactly the way they had rehearsed it time and time again.

Finch started the truck and rolled it forward a few yards until its nose was in the middle of the street. Then he put it in reverse and cut the wheel sharply left and backed over the curb and onto the sidewalk. Finch turned the ignition off, put the keys in his pocket, and got out to admire his handiwork.

The van's back doors overlapped the first of approximately fifteen rather steep steps.

"I think I got it an inch too far left," Finch said, grinning.

Because he had driven the last few blocks against the grain—as it were—and had then aligned the back of the truck with the steps on the first try, they still had four minutes to kill.

Trout bored one of the minutes to death by making certain that Finch hadn't left the keys in the truck, which could have been catastrophic, all right. Somebody would have had to reach in and get them and might have put an eye out on the gearshift knob or got his head caught in the steering wheel.

Finch showed Trout the keys, snapped his fingers, and said, "It's going to go like *that*."

The heavy air didn't let the *snap!* drift off.

Trout jumped and looked up at an apartment building that was directly across from the Thirty-third Precinct.

Nobody looked out.

No new lights came on.

"I was hoping it would go quieter," Trout said.

"It's going to go like *that*."

Finch snapped his fingers again, but without making any noise. When he rotated his wrist, a ring flew off his right hand. The ring bounced on the sidewalk three or four times and rolled underneath the back of the van.

Finch said, "That's my high school graduation ring."

"You might ought to get it," Trout told him.

Finch got down on his hands and knees and then on his stomach. He slithered underneath the truck and felt through some tiny puddles of water for his ring and caught the back of his jump suit on some kind of bolt by the drive shaft.

It was no big deal.

Trout grabbed Finch's feet and pulled him backwards until the jump suit came free.

While Finch felt for his ring with a stick, Trout walked to the back of the truck and opened the doors a couple of inches.

"It's me," he whispered. "We're here. Finch dropped his high school graduation ring under the truck, and he's fishing it out."

"Well, for God's sake," a woman said.

Trout closed the doors and knelt down to see how Finch was doing.

"Got it," Finch said.

"Where's the gas tank on this thing?" Trout asked.

Finch quickly closed the lid on the cigarette lighter he had been using to see with.

After Finch wiped off some grease he had picked up rolling around under the truck, he put his high school graduation ring on his thumb so it wouldn't sail off again at an inopportune time, and he and Trout walked through the front doors of the Thirty-third Precinct.

The doors were glass with aluminum frames. Nothing else nearby was as modern.

Trout and Finch wore bushy beards that glued on and steamed off. They carried clipboards.

They walked to the desk officer with as much confidence as was possible under the circumstances.

The Thirty-third Precinct was an old building with wooden floors and plastered walls and high ceilings. It didn't sound like Trout and Finch were walking. It sounded like they were stomping. Their footsteps echoed all over the place.

They went straight to the front desk, where Trout smiled and said "Hi."

The desk officer sat at a slightly elevated platform. His name was House. There was an old round clock on the wall behind him. There was a sign to his left that said *Detectives*. There was an arrow next to the sign that pointed down some stairs. Trout glanced at the stairs and was pleased by their darkness.

"How bad is it?" Sergeant House asked, looking up and then back down at some paperwork.

The question caught Trout off guard. He scratched his chin, which didn't need it. "Well, it's misting out there."

"Not that, what you're here for," Sergeant House said, heaving himself to a softer spot on his chair. He was fat.

"It's not bad, it's good," Trout said.

"Is this some sort of practical joke?"

"We don't do that kind of thing to people with guns." Trout continued to smile but felt sneaky doing it.

"You're telling me," Sergeant House said, shifting again in his chair, "that you have good news at this time of night?"

"No, it's great," Finch said.

He, too, was smiling.

Finch's smile impressed Trout as being the kind displayed at the checkout counter by a person with some T-bone steaks stuffed down his pants. The smile seemed phony.

"Hang on a second," Sergeant House said. He returned his attention to the paper in front of him and spoke as he made some notes. He told Trout and Finch about the man who had come in five minutes before. The man was in a robe, carrying a jar.

Trout nodded absentmindedly.

Finch nodded, genuinely interested.

"There's pissants in the jar, eight or nine of the things," Sergeant House said, looking up occasionally to see how his story was being received. "They're red, like little crabs."

"You're kidding," Finch said.

Trout rubbed his eyes and wondered how things were going so far. You can only practice so much. You can practice backing and loading and escaping. But you can't prepare yourself for time consuming stories about people with jars of ants. Although Finch was positive that their success was predestined because eliminating the police from the picture was such a tremendous idea, Trout still had a hunch they were going to have to work for their millions. What, for example, was going to keep this desk officer from telling story after story after story?

"This man with the jar," Sergeant House said to Finch, who was so interested he was almost taking notes, "claims his wife is putting the pissants in his bed, in between the sheets and in the pillowcases, four or five a night, trying to drive him crazy. This guy wants his wife arrested, so I have to fill out the forms."

"Unbelievable," Finch said. "What's his name?"

"Pock. How's that for a name?"

"Not so good," Finch said.

"It's amazing how some people look like their names, you know?" Sergeant House turned over a form and began writing on the back.

"What did this Pock look like?" Finch asked.

"Skinny, like a weasel. And he had bad skin."

No, Trout thought as the desk officer showed Finch the complaint filed by the man who claimed his wife was putting ants in his bed, a good idea does not guarantee wealth. A good idea simply gets you in the front door. Once inside, they were not supposed to set up housekeeping. They were supposed to keep moving. Trout decided he should have written out what they were supposed to say to the desk officer on index cards.

"It's the mist," Sergeant House was saying to Finch, who was nodding some more. "Most people think it's the moon that brings out the lunatics. But I've been doing this for eighteen years. It's fog and drizzle that makes a person put pissants on her husband."

"You people do a hell of a job," Finch said.

"We try."

Before they could start showing each other snapshots of their relatives, Trout cleared his throat and said, "We're here about the chair."

"Hey," Finch said, winking. "This is a busy man. Let him fill out his form. We got all night."

Trout frowned.

Finch winked again.

Sergeant House wrote some more.

14

Finch had recently graduated with honors from a power-of-positive-thinking seminar—honors and a paid-in-full receipt for four hundred dollars. And ever since the graduation exercises, which took five minutes because there were only ten students, Finch had been walking around with a silly grin on his face. Once he had his diploma, he thought that if you wanted something badly enough, all you had to do was grit your teeth and will it to happen. Finch's good mood—his positive outlook on life in general and this project in particular—was starting to give Trout a headache that flowed forward like lava to points over each eye.

Finch got a drink of water from a fountain by the stairs. He attempted to whistle casually.

Trout watched the clock.

"Okay," Sergeant House said, sliding the form aside. "How much do you want for it?"

"For what?," Trout asked.

"That chair."

"Nothing."

Sergeant House put his pencil down and said he didn't have much of a sense of humor between the hours of 11 P.M. and 7 A.M.

"We have," Trout said, starting again, "a new chair for you." He consulted his clipboard on which nothing was written. "All the desk officers are getting new equipment, starting with the chairs."

Sergeant House slapped his desk. A pencil jumped. Trout jumped.

"You mean to tell me I get a new chair after only four years of begging?"

"It's leather," Finch said. "I rode over in the back with it. It's unbelievable. It's the size of a hot tub. It feels like there's mashed potatoes in the cushions."

Sergeant House nodded and hauled himself to his feet. He

rolled his current chair off the platform and shoved it into a corner. It was a cheap chair, covered with vinyl. Stuffing was sticking out of three or four holes. "What kind of leather is it?"

"Brown," Finch said. "There's a little handle on the side. You turn it and everything starts vibrating."

Sergeant House said he was not sure that movers were supposed to take joyrides on city property.

"Sorry," Finch said.

"Forget it," Sergeant House said.

He put his arms around the two of them, and they all went to get the new leather chair.

Sergeant House was fifty-four years old and he hadn't ridden the Exercycle he had received for a birthday in six years; consequently the first thing he did after looking into the back of the large truck was breathe deeply.

The Exercycle, which was at the foot of the bed, had clothes hangers on the handlebars. It was being used as an extra closet.

After Sergeant House took three deep breaths, he watched the pulse on his left wrist hop around like a jumping bean.

He was about the only one in his apartment building who had not had his heart fixed. His next-door neighbor went in to have a sore throat checked, and he came out with a chest that looked like electric trains had been running over it.

Once Sergeant House got a reasonably steady heartbeat established, he did his best to look helpless. He let his head and shoulders sag. Although he didn't come into contact with criminals too often, except when a drunk ran up from the holding cell and tried to escape, he frequently had coffee and doughnuts with people who messed around with criminals all the time. And he knew that a grandstand play against overwhelming odds was a good way to wind up starring in a funeral. The way the book said you were supposed to react in times of great peril was calmly. You were supposed to

16

observe details that could be helpful in the arrest and subsequent prosecution of the bastards who had you. You were supposed to remain alert and wait quietly for help to arrive.

There was no leather chair in the back of the truck.

There were two people in there instead, a man and a woman. The man was monstrously proportioned—he was at least six-seven—so Sergeant House decided once and for all that any kind of loosely constructed counterattack would be in very poor taste.

It would taste like blood.

When Sergeant House opened the back doors on the truck, Roebuck, the big one, was on him in about two seconds.

Roebuck was wearing a police uniform, and that temporarily froze Sergeant House, not that he would have had much of a chance if Roebuck had been wearing a dress.

Roebuck leaped out of the truck and got Sergeant House in a bear hug and lifted him a good foot off the ground.

Annabel, the woman, who had a nice figure for a crook, took Sergeant House's blackjack, which he used for a paperweight.

They also took his billfold, loose change, pen, keys, and shoes. He felt like an El Dorado that had been left on the street for a quarter of an hour on a Saturday night.

They stripped him in about forty-five seconds.

"I got the chrome," Finch said, taking Sergeant House's handcuffs.

After they took Sergeant House's belongings, Roebuck hoisted him into the truck as though he were a toddler.

"Don't move or you'll be sorry," Roebuck said.

Sergeant House nodded and looked around for clues. The truck was the size of a moving van, but it didn't have any writing on the outside, which should have been a tip-off.

Sergeant House didn't find any clues. He found a wall and leaned against it and wondered how in the world they had discovered the twenty-thousand-dollar nest egg he had put together over in Queens as divorce insurance. It stood to reason that one of the people at the bank must have put this kidnapping together. Still and all, it seemed to be a lot of work and a big risk for a ransom payoff of twenty grand, split at least four ways.

"She doesn't know about it," Sergeant House said as Trout climbed into the truck and pulled the back doors to within a couple of inches of closed.

Trout carried a flashlight, which he turned on and put on the floor.

"It's carried under Edgar Merriweather. But then, you people know that, don't you?"

"What is?" Trout asked.

"The account."

Trout tied a shoelace and wondered if he was getting the flu. It was as though he had some sort of learning disability. He could hear the words all right, but they didn't have any depth, any continuity.

"So what you're going to have to do to get at the account is tell Gladys. Do me one favor, okay?"

Trout rubbed the back of his neck and moved his head in small circles.

"Tell her I put it away for a second honeymoon, okay? We're not getting along so good. She might bring a suitcase full of meat loaf to the drop site. The key is, tell her it was going to be a big surprise."

"Tell who what?"

"Thank God I opened the account in Queens as Mr. *and Mrs.* Merriweather. That way Gladys can get at it. She's going to have to tell them at the bank she's *Mrs. Merriweather*, though. I did the Mrs. Merriweather signature with my left hand. The account card is taped to the bottom of the third dresser drawer on the left-hand side."

Trout looked at his watch.

"Have Gladys practice the Mrs. Merriweather signature.

I opened it Mr. and Mrs. so it wouldn't look like I was hiding anything."

"Who's Gladys?"

"She's my wife."

"Oh," Trout said. "Then who's Mrs. Merriweather?"

"The wife in Queens."

"I thought your name was House."

"It is," Sergeant House said.

"Hang on a second." Trout walked to the back doors and stuck his head out. All was well. His three associates were on the steps in front of the police station. Finch had taken the sawhorse with the Wet Paint sign to the top of the stairs. Trout gave them the okay signal, filled his lungs with cool, moist air, and returned to where what's-his-name was sitting on the floor.

"Starting now, we don't want to hear a sound from inside this van."

"The only sound you could possibly hear is me dropping dead."

"Then sit in the corner so you won't fall."

Sergeant House crawled to one of the front corners, as instructed.

"If we hear a sound, it will be the last one."

"You don't have anything to worry about in that department."

"Fine," Trout said.

He turned and walked toward the doors.

"Be sure and tell my wife I love her," Sergeant House said.

"Which one?" Trout asked.

"My first wife is dead."

"Well then, if you make a sound, you can tell her."

And with that, Trout turned and climbed out of the truck, wishing as he jumped onto the steps that he had a program so he could follow this story line a little better.

He lifted himself onto the rear bumper and locked the

doors with a key and wondered if his brain was getting enough oxygen.

Trout and Finch got into the front seat of the truck, with Finch behind the wheel.

Annabel and Roebuck escorted them and stood by the driver's door.

Trout, who had tried to place his mind in the middle of a calm sea as Finch had suggested, was still thinking of ten or so things at once. He leaned forward in his seat and spoke first to Roebuck. He told him that his shirttail was out in the back.

"His shirttail is also wet," Annabel said.

She was ready to get on with it.

Trout, however, was ready to think and talk a little. They had a minute and forty-five seconds. This was the last chance they would have to reflect together; from now on they would simply react to whatever the wind blew their way. Trout believed that there was no substitute for serious thought. And who could argue with him? He had, after all, thought of *this*.

"Now, you simply have to watch your temper," he said.

Roebuck wiped some moisture off his nose.

Annabel looked around impatiently.

"Which one of us are you talking to?" Roebuck asked.

"You," Trout said.

"You've got my word on it."

"I mean it. If you hit anybody, it's going to throw everything off rhythm."

"Okay," Roebuck said.

Annabel wondered what Trout wanted Roebuck to do—take a blood oath?

"I want him to *think* about it."

"I am," Roebuck said, tucking in his shirttail.

Annabel told Trout that all he was doing was making everybody nervous.

"We need to think about any little things that could cause trouble," Trout said.

"Like *what* little things?" Finch asked.

"Bullets," Trout said, looking him directly in the eye.

They thought about bullets, those hollow-pointed jobs that exploded like hand grenades upon contact with bones, until it was time for Finch to move the truck away from the front steps. He put the van in first gear and rolled forward, carefully dropping the tires off the curb so the passenger, Sergeant House, wouldn't be thrown into the air. Finch made a slow right and proceeded cautiously toward the intersection. He stopped at a red light, which was only about seventy-five yards from the precinct's front steps. A cab went past. That was it.

"Hey," Roebuck yelled as Finch waited for the cab to move out of sight. "I just thought of one of those little things we never talked about."

Roebuck and Annabel had walked halfway up the front steps.

Finch had just begun a sweet right turn.

"Stop the truck," Trout said. "Pull to the curb."

Finch did that.

"Pull *off* the curb."

Finch did that.

"What happens if somebody surrenders to me?" Roebuck asked.

"Huh?" Trout said. He leaned out the passenger window.

Roebuck cupped his hands around his mouth and shouted, "What do I do if somebody walks in off the street and wants to give himself up?"

"That's not a half-bad question," Finch said after a couple of seconds.

"Did you hear that?" a woman in an apartment across from the Thirty-third Precinct asked her husband.

"Hear what?"

They were watching television in their bedroom four stories up.

"Somebody outside is yelling about surrendering."

"I didn't hear anything," the man said.

The woman got up and walked to the window.

"Stay away from there," her husband said. "There might be some kind of shoot-out. You might get killed."

The woman peeked around the curtains.

"Nobody will surrender," Trout yelled at Roebuck.

"But what if they do?"

"Take them."

"*Take* them? You don't mean take them *out*? You don't mean *kill* them?"

"For God's sake, no," Trout shouted back. "*Accept* them. Put them somewhere. But it won't happen. We'll talk about this later."

"There's a big cop yelling at a truck about killing somebody," the woman in the apartment said.

"It's probably some kind of maneuver," her husband guessed. "Some kind of field work."

"I thought you said moving to a place across from a precinct house was *smart*. I'm going to call the police."

"You don't see any burglars, do you?" said the man in the apartment across from the Thirty-third Precinct.

"I don't know," his wife answered. "That's what I'm going to find out."

She called the police.

It didn't take long.

She opened the window and called out:

"Hey down there."

"Go," Trout said to Finch. "Before they get our license number."

Finch moved the van forward and out of sight.

The woman in the window wanted to know what the hell was going on.

22

"Nothing," Annabel yelled up.

"You some kind of policewoman?"

"Yeah," Annabel said.

"What's the business with the truck all about?"

"It was parked by a hydrant."

"You're going to *kill* somebody for parking by a hydrant?"

"We were talking about killing the engine."

"I'm with you a hundred percent," the woman's husband said. He struck his head out the window. "You let the bastards park by a fire hydrant, the next thing you know, they're in here gutting all the apartments."

"You might be a little quieter this time of night," the woman said, closing the window.

"This is exactly the kind of thing you get for thinking too much," Annabel told Roebuck.

Annabel and Roebuck went into the lobby of the police station and tiptoed to the desk.

"This is eerie," Roebuck said. All you could hear was the clock ticking.

He retrieved the cheap chair that Sergeant House had rolled off into a corner and carried it back to the platform. He adjusted a lever on the chair so that he wouldn't be too tall for the desk.

"We really *should* have brought a leather chair," Roebuck said, settling himself in. "How do I look?"

"I'd feel very secure as a victim. You look like you're in complete control from the word go."

"No kidding," Roebuck said, sitting up straighter. He stacked some paper in front of him in neat rows. "Why don't we go ahead and run through it?"

"Okay," Annabel said.

Roebuck turned around and looked up at the clock. They were on time. During this brief slack period if somebody wandered upstairs, which was unlikely because of the meeting

23

that had just started below, they had some options. Actually, they had two choices. Annabel would tell anybody trying to use the stairs that there was wet paint all over. And if that didn't work, Roebuck would club whoever walked on up.

"You all set?" Annabel asked.

"I'm ready," Roebuck said, arranging some pencils.

Annabel walked a few steps toward the front door, lowered her head, and returned to Roebuck's desk.

"Somebody just mugged me," she said quietly.

"Fill out a form."

For an instant Annabel wondered if being a multimillionairess was going to be worth it. It wouldn't be worth it if she had to spend all the profits on medication and specialists. Being rich would be fun only if she could enjoy it in good mental health.

She smiled at Roebuck, who was holding out a piece of paper and a pencil with no lead. Roebuck was a terrific fellow. He was loyal. He was courageous. He was big. He just wasn't known for his finesse.

"Listen," Annabel said. She took the piece of paper and returned it to the stack of forms.

"It's the right one," Roebuck said. "It's an all-purpose complaint form, just like the one Trout stole from here and showed us."

Annabel nodded and patted one of Roebuck's big mitts. "Getting mugged is a very emotional experience. It's terrifying. It's usually done by dope addicts. It's violent. So if somebody comes in with that kind of problem, you need to use a little more compassion. Before you hand somebody a form, you need to say you're sorry or something."

Roebuck shrugged. "It's just hard for me to imagine not creaming somebody who did that to you. And then on the other hand, it was just practice."

"Right," Annabel said.

"So other than that, how did it go?"

24

"Except for no lead in the pencil, swell."

"What if somebody comes in with something like a murder?"

"They won't *walk* a murder in. They'd call it in. I'd handle that. All you do, no matter what comes in, is hand them a form."

"And say I'm sorry."

"You don't have to say it in so many words. Just *act* like you're sorry."

Roebuck attempted a sorrowful expression. He looked as if he had just taken a bite out of a lemon.

"Just hand them a form," Annabel said.

While those two went over the process of handing out forms one more time, Trout and Finch maneuvered the truck around the block.

Sergeant House sat quietly in the back. He held his breath and listened for a big splash.

"Be careful," Trout said absentmindedly as Finch waited for a light to change.

"There's nothing to hit except buildings," Finch replied. The mist was heavier. Visibility was only a few blocks. There was nothing on the street except an occasional taxi and one dog that limped. Finch wished for a little thunder, then the light changed in their favor and he executed a simple right turn.

Although they would have gone tonight even if the stars were out, light drizzle like this was preferred because it kept even the drunks indoors. Another reason there was nobody out and around was the neighborhood, which was virtually closed. This area was about eighty percent offices.

As Finch rolled the van around to the back, signaling like crazy, Trout had to admit that things looked good enough. But there was more to it than that. Things had to feel good too. And Trout still felt funny.

"Stop a second," he said.

Finch sighed, signaled right, and stopped in front of a department store. "What is it?"

"I keep thinking I've forgotten something."

"The only thing you've forgotten is how to enjoy the scenery."

Trout wondered if maybe that was the problem: Maybe they had gone over this part too predictably. Maybe what they needed to do was go over it differently. "Let's think about it, starting from the other end, working our way back."

"At the positive-thinking seminar," Finch said, "this was called letting life get the best of you."

While Trout was thinking backwards from the museum, Finch did his part. He was going to buy himself an island with his millions, one where they dropped newspapers and TV dinners from an airplane once a month. When he closed his eyes, all he could see was half-naked girls playing volleyball. Finch was the referee. "Let's play that point over," he envisioned himself saying.

"It's perfect any way you look at it," Finch said, restarting the van and moving it slowly through the drizzle.

Trout looked at his right palm and wiped some ink off his life line.

"The first thing you do," Finch said of the positive-thinking seminar that had turned his life around, "is clear your mind. Think of blackness." He turned the windshield wipers on. "Tell me when you've done that."

Trout humored Finch—it was that or choke him—so he nodded.

"Now then, the secret of positive thinking is where you replace a bad thought with a good one. Some guys at the seminar had a lot of luck thinking about the first time they had sex."

Trout winced.

"Or the last time," Finch said.

26

"How about the *middle* time?" Trout asked.

"*Now* you've got the hang of it. Thinking is supposed to be fun."

They moved on around the block, and Finch did his best to get Trout loosened up and in a better frame of mind. He told Trout that in the next few hours they would find out whether they were going to be wealthy the rest of their lives, or worthless bums; whether they were going to live right, or whether they were going to die.

Trout sighed six times in two blocks.

Finch drove through an alley, parked in a loading zone, and killed the engine.

They were behind the police station and in the middle of three dozen or more squad cars. The majority of the police cars were parked under a cement slab. The area behind the Thirty-third Precinct was considerably more active than it was out front.

Every minute or so, somebody came out the back door in civilian clothes and got into a regular car and drove off. These were police officers and detectives. They had completed a shift and had showered.

The average officer leaving the Thirty-third Precinct by the back door was very young. It looked like there had been a fraternity meeting inside. The majority of the officers had moustaches. Finch thought it seemed like somebody in there was trying to create a master race, like Lawrence Welk's singers.

One of the young officers wandered by the truck and said "Hi" to Finch.

"Hi," Finch said.

"We're going to deliver a little furniture once the shift has changed," Trout said.

"We going to get our pool table?" the officer asked.

Trout told him it was only desks and chairs.

27

"You might ought to leave somebody in the truck at all times so it won't get stolen," the young officer said.

The three of them had a nice laugh about that.

"They're overmatched," Finch said when the policeman was out of range.

"They're a little better than they look."

"They look eighteen," Finch said. "I got a plant that's eighteen."

Trout nodded.

He had put together a comprehensive study of the Thirty-third Precinct and the men and women who worked there, and he thought about their weaknesses as the officers wandered to their cars.

Trout knew, for example, that during the late shift on a weeknight, an average of only 2.5 people walked in off the street with a complaint. On a *wet* weeknight the average dropped to 1.5. Trout knew that, because he had sat across the way counting. He had rented a $775-a-month efficiency facing the Thirty-third Precinct and had counted customers for the worst part of three months. The very worst part was between three A.M. and five A.M. when there was hardly anybody around except derelicts who crawled up the steps to get out of the weather.

Trout had also frequented a neighborhood bar where officers from the Thirty-third Precinct drank, and after several dozen casual conversations he had put together a fascinating professional and psychological profile.

Trout had bought a couple of rounds here and there and decided never to take a hostage and try to wade through police lines, holding a knife at the hostage's throat.

The police were very good at picking off people who did that.

They were also terrific at staking out a liquor store after it had been robbed ten straight nights, and they towed away cars with the best of them. After many nights of mingling,

Trout concluded that the police were damned decent at what they did, which was to arrest blockheads.

Trout learned as much about the average criminal as he did about the average police man or woman.

The average criminal was unbelievably dull.

Consequently, Trout became comfortable with the premise that the police could be lulled into a false sense of security by anyone who used the head on his shoulders as something other than a battering ram. The average thinking man or woman, it seemed, devoted his or her time and energies to stock frauds, price fixing, oil swindling, and various other types of corporate corruption. That left a lot of room for some people to make a great deal of money on the street, in the trenches, if they were not afraid to roll up their sleeves and get their hands dirty.

Beat cops and detectives, particularly those who worked the night shift, were used to competing with guys who had four teeth, guys who had dropped out of junior high, virtual morons.

Furthermore, when an officer passed out drunk on the job or shot an innocent bystander, the officer, Trout learned, was transferred to a graveyard shift to work out the kinks. The average police-person who worked weird hours was very overrated.

One out of every hundred or so joined the force to serve mankind. And these select few generally wound up wounded or worse. The courts were so fouled up that serving mankind was out of the question, so after about a month on the job even the most dedicated officer was forced to rethink his or her priorities.

Instead of serving mankind, they wound up serving themselves.

About the only surefire way a police officer could make this a better country in which to live was by staying alive, getting a pension, and investing a little something in the stock market.

So after more than two months of extensive research, Trout decided he would be more than willing to trade shots in the dark with the graveyard shift at the Thirty-third Precinct.

Finch had a point. The most important elements, from the weather to surprise, seemed to be in their favor.

He and Trout waited in the truck a couple of minutes longer than they had planned, to make sure everybody from the previous shift was out of the building. They didn't want to have to steal somebody who was due home.

Sergeant House was in a better mood when the van stopped and he heard the two doors up front slam shut. The walls of the van were surprisingly thick, but he could make out the sounds of doors closing.

His pulse was near normal because he had figured this out.

It was a joke.

Some of his co-workers were always teasing him about the painless job he had. When he went off duty in the morning, he usually received a few pats on the back for having guarded the clock and water fountain with such aplomb.

So what a few of his fellow officers had obviously done was to hire these comedians to pretend to kidnap him.

That was pretty funny, all right.

But he was not a desk officer for nothing. All those years of sitting around reading mysteries with trick endings had prepared Sergeant House for a problem like this.

He was going to lie down and pretend to be dead when the doors were finally opened.

The plan was to get the police when they were all together and surprise them. Beyond that, the plan was very flexible. Had somebody tried this once before, Trout could have gone over the court records and corrected the mistakes. But since they were breaking new ground, they had to make one reasonable assumption—that the police would not expect somebody to take them from their home base—and wing it.

Trout and Finch sat quietly for five minutes after the light in the locker room went off.

Then they walked in through the back entrance and stood in the hallway, listening. The locker room was the first door to the left. Finch stuck his head inside and heard some water dripping.

They stood by the back door about a minute so their eyes and stomachs could adjust to the dimness.

Trout nodded to himself, pleased at the quiet, and led the way to the other end of the hall. He stopped a few yards from the door to the ready room and whispered, "Don't shoot unless it's absolutely necessary. And whatever you do, don't shoot me."

"I believe I can handle that," Finch said, grinning.

Trout took a deep breath, swung open the door to the ready room, and stepped inside. Finch moved in behind Trout and took a couple of steps along a wall.

The ready room was where the police found out whom they were going to attempt to arrest that morning, and how badly the Knicks got beat.

Lieutenant Bush was in charge of this routine. He had just given the Knicks' score and was starting to discuss some prostitutes when Trout and Finch showed up unannounced. Lieutenant Bush glanced sideways from his podium and said, "How's it going?"

The commanding officer's friendliness temporarily froze Trout, who had his hand inside a gunnysack with his finger around the trigger of a machine gun.

"Okay," Trout lied.

It was not going anywhere near that well. A string that

ran around the top of the gunnysack had become tangled on the butt of the machine gun and Trout was having a terrible time working the weapon free.

"What's in there?" Lieutenant Bush asked.

Trout tried to pull the cord off the gun butt and succeeded only in closing the top of the gunny sack around his right forearm. This was obviously another of those goddamn parts that an extra month of practice couldn't have made perfect.

"Let me give you a hand." Lieutenant Bush put his cup of coffee on the podium.

"I got it," Trout said. He pointed the machine gun at the floor and stepped on the end of the gunnysack with his right foot. He worked the gun free by yanking the cord out of its stitching. He threw the cord aside and emptied the gun out of the sack onto the floor.

Lieutenant Bush looked disbelievingly at Trout and turned back toward his people to ask, "All right, who ordered a machine gun?"

"The guy before you did," an officer in the front row said. "Four years ago."

Quite a few people laughed.

"Excuse me a second," Trout said to Lieutenant Bush.

"Sure thing. Listen, is there anything I have to sign for the gun?"

Trout said that the receipt was in the truck, and he motioned for Finch to join him back in the hallway. Finch, who had his hand around a pistol in the right front pocket of his jump suit, backed out of the room, which looked a little peculiar.

Trout moved away from the door and said quietly, "They're not surprised."

"Knock that one up front on the head and I'll cover you from the back of the room."

Trout told Finch to keep his voice down. That the police

weren't surprised was a compliment, as strange as it seemed. They weren't surprised, but they weren't on their guard either. They were so relaxed, nothing short of violence would convince them they were in trouble. "I'll talk to the one at the podium and have him get the message across to the others."

"What the hell are we going to do, *debate* them?" Finch said.

"We're playing it safe."

Trout told Finch to have a seat in the back row and stay alert.

"Nobody is going to believe this," Finch said.

He returned to the ready room and sat at the end of the last row next to an older uniformed officer who asked how he was doing. Finch said that he had no earthly idea. The officer said there was a lot of that going around, and asked Finch for some help with a crossword puzzle.

Once Finch was seated, Trout asked Lieutenant Bush for a word in the hallway. The lieutenant brought his coffee with him. He held the saucer in his left hand and the cup in his right hand. If Trout could keep from being kicked or bitten, he would be in good shape.

"We're not delivering this gun," he said.

"Is it somebody's birthday?"

Trout found it almost impossible to believe that he was having such a difficult time making the simplest point. Upstairs the fat desk officer hadn't understood about the chair, then he'd begun rambling about an assortment of women who had nothing to do with anything. Now they thought his gun was chocolate.

"I doubt it," Trout said about the birthday.

"You're not with one of those singing telegram companies?"

"Listen to me. We're not with anybody. We've come to get you people."

"Get us. What do you mean, *get* us?"

33

"It means this," Trout said.

He took Lieutenant Bush's gun out of its shoulder holster.

Although Lieutenant Bush had commanded the graveyard shift at the Thirty-third Precinct for the last three years, masterminding such projects as raids on whorehouses and bookie joints, he had in his first few years with the department, before his marriage, worked at two other precincts, including one on the upper west side of town that was populated by dangerous people, some of whom had adjoining scars from gang fights. Once, Lieutenant Bush had arrested four people whose chests, when the men were lined up next to one another, looked like a graph of the Dow Jones Industrial Average. They had been damaged by the same knife stroke.

The man with the machine gun, and now his pistol, reminded Lieutenant Bush of a criminal.

The majority of the officers working at the Thirty-third Precinct were relatives of public officials. They were given lengthy tours there because their loved ones didn't want to see them dead before they came to their senses and quit to become stockbrokers. And whereas Lieutenant Bush was himself the mayor's cousin-in-law and as complacent as the rest of them, he nevertheless remembered what the outside world was like and realized that this was not a delivery, a singing birthday greeting, or a prank.

So he did as he was told.

He went back to the podium and made one more announcement.

He told his people that unless they put their hands up, he was going to be target practice for the man who had a clear shot at him from the hallway.

"It's about *time*," Finch said. "Don't anybody move."

"No, have them put their hands up first," Trout said from the hallway.

"What the hell is going on here?" an officer in the front row asked.

"We're being robbed," Lieutenant Bush said.

"Oh, my God." The older officer at the back closed his eyes.

Finch helped the older officer, whose name was Billows, raise his hands.

Finch took Billows's gun and told Trout that they should have brought along some oxygen and stretchers for the ones over eighty.

As the graveyard shift sat quietly but irritably with their hands on their heads, Lieutenant Bush composed himself and requested another minute in private with Trout.

The two of them walked away from the podium.

Finch collected some more guns.

"This isn't bad," Lieutenant Bush said, "walking right in here to rob us."

"What is it you want?" Trout asked.

Lieutenant Bush decided to play it straight because a lot was at stake. "This is a great place to work," he said, glancing out of the corner of his eye at his people. "There's not a lot of what you would call life-threatening crime going on around here during the early morning hours. There's an average number of stolen vehicles, some breaking and entering, some gambling."

"That's nice," Trout said.

Lieutenant Bush asked Trout what he knew about the way the city, in its official, conglomerate sense, worked.

"Speed this up," Trout said. If these people wanted to think they were being robbed, fine; anything that promoted cooperation was worth tolerating for a few seconds.

"The bigger the screw-up, the closer to Times Square they send you."

"What exactly do you want?"

"If this gets out," Lieutenant Bush whispered, "we'll all wind up policing bathhouses. We love it here. We love this old building and this neighborhood and the cars out back. We love the air. We've got some picnic tables up on the roof. This is our *home.*"

"We haven't got time for this."

"Let's not allow what's happened here to get beyond this room."

Trout frowned.

"The valuables can go, of course. These things happen. We'll all be the better for it. Let's leave it at that."

"You're asking us to keep our mouths shut?"

"I would appreciate it."

Trout told Lieutenant Bush he would cancel the ad thanking the police department for its support that he had planned to have published on Sunday.

Finch carried two gunnysacks through the rows of folding chairs.

There were fourteen police officers sitting with their hands on their heads.

Finch put the guns and clubs and handcuffs in one sack, and the valuables in the other.

He made the rounds routinely until an officer named Buck who was seated at the end of the front row said through clenched teeth, "We'll get you for this."

Finch dropped Buck's gun into the appropriate sack, turned to Trout, and asked if he had ever heard worse last words. He returned his attention to Buck and squinted at his name tag. "*We'll get you for this* stinks, Buck. You want to try for something more sentimental, something that rhymes?"

"I meant what I said."

"Easy, Buck," Lieutenant Bush said.

"Listen," Finch said to Buck, who was wearing a baseball cap and the obligatory moustache. "Don't take this so hard. If you get fired, you can always be a night watchman out at Yankee Stadium. You'd be right at home with that hat."

"Let's go," Trout said.

"Hang on a second," Finch called over his shoulder. "We've got a conflict here. My personality is conflicting with this guy's moustache."

Buck squinted and appeared to consider lashing out at Finch with his fists.

"If you don't straighten up, Buck, I'm going to take your baseball cap. The girls love it, right? I'm going to stuff it down a sewer. You ever play any *real* ball, Buck, any organized ball?"

Buck looked up at the bill of his cap. He enjoyed wearing it very much. As a matter of fact, a couple of women *had* found the ball cap, which had 33rd on the front, rather entertaining.

"You never played any ball. Only ex-ball players should get to wear baseball caps, not cab drivers and garbage collectors and cops."

"I played some intramural ball," Buck said.

"That's horseshit, that's sissy ball. That doesn't count. If you want to keep that cap, you better behave yourself."

Finch reached out and turned up the bill of Buck's baseball cap. "You're on probation. Now you don't look like a ball player. You look like a sap."

Finch finished his rounds without any more back talk.

Trout got on the telephone that was in the corner of the ready room and dialed the front desk. He told Annabel that things were under control.

She said "Good" and hung up.

She left Roebuck with his forms and desire to succeed and went to the communications room—one flight up from the lobby—where Heather, the communications officer, was sitting at a computer bank reading *Cosmopolitan*. Her back was to the door, and, she was wearing a headset. A couple of police radios were chirping routinely about things going on

37

in other, livelier neighborhoods. Heather was lost in a story about how you got points for having sex in unusual places. You got two points for having sex on a conveyor belt. You got three points for having sex on a city bus. And so on. This *Cosmo,* it was some piece of work. It made Heather feel sheltered.

Annabel tapped the communications officer on the shoulder with the end of a pistol and told her to get up.

Heather dropped the magazine and asked, "What is this?"

"A drill," Annabel said.

"What are we practicing?"

"How to retire gracefully."

Annabel glanced at the computers and recognized most of the models.

She told Heather that she would be okay unless she thought or spoke; then she led the communications officer down the two flights of stairs to where Trout and Finch held the rest of the Thirty-third Precinct motionless.

When Annabel went by Roebuck's floor, they waved at each other.

Roebuck had great news. Nobody had walked in off the street with so much as a purse snatching to report.

Trout met Annabel in the downstairs hallway and asked how it was going with Roebuck.

"It's quiet. How about here?"

"See for yourself."

Annabel had Heather sit by Buck, who was in a very bad mood. Buck was frowning so hard that when he relaxed his brow his baseball cap almost popped off his head.

"Welcome to church," Finch said.

Annabel nodded.

Trout checked his watch.

Finch took Annabel aside and explained that the police thought they were being robbed. He asked Trout what he was supposed to do with the stuff in the sacks.

"Put their guns in a locker," Trout whispered. "But don't leave *our* guns in there, okay?"

The three of them stood a few seconds without speaking.

The precinct was officially theirs, and everybody was having a bit of difficulty accepting the ease with which the takeover had been accomplished.

Finch stuffed the sacks of guns into a locker and walked through the mist to the truck, his footsteps bouncing off the cement. Then he learned a little lesson about overconfidence.

It was too still for words, outside.

When Finch cleared his throat, it sounded like an avalanche.

He climbed in behind the wheel, pulled the door to without banging any latches together, and put on his gloves. Gloves didn't leave fingerprints. He looked around the front seat for anything that could be traced. He picked up a candy-bar wrapper and stuffed it into his front pocket.

Finch closed his eyes and started the motor.

The noise was deafening. It sounded like jackhammers.

He pulled the truck out of the loading zone and past the rear door, preparing to back up. He didn't have much room to work with. It took Finch four tries to align the rear of the van with the single back door. On the first try he was off to the left by a couple of yards.

"What the hell are you doing?" Trout asked from the hallway.

"Sorry," Finch said.

He pulled forward and finally got the rear doors snugly against the back entrance to the Thirty-third Precinct. He got out and wondered why in the world he had done that. With the truck flush against the building, there was no room for him to get inside.

"Hey," Trout yelled from the hallway.

"Yeah," Finch answered.

39

"The damn truck doors are still closed."

Finch said he would fix things. He'd pull the truck away from the building and measure the width of the doors. Then he'd stop the right distance away so that the people could be loaded without anybody from a nearby building being able to see them walk, even a few feet.

"Finch?"

"What?"

"Is this some sort of joke?"

"What?"

"There's no need to do that. Just pull up and prop the doors all the way open and back flush against the building."

"How do I get back inside?"

"You crawl under the damn truck."

"Okay."

Trout told Finch it would be a shame to achieve something as complicated as capturing an entire police squad and then ruin it by backing an empty truck through a goddamn building.

Finch apologized and said he would start concentrating again.

With the truck finally in place, they loaded the members of the graveyard shift into the back of the van.

That came as quite a surprise.

Heather, the communications officer, asked if they were going to be mass-murdered.

Trout told her to quit whining.

Lieutenant Bush was at first puzzled and then furious. He took one hand off his head, pointed at Trout, and said that all bets were off unless this loading was stopped immediately. "I thought you were going to *rob* us."

"We did," Trout said.

"Then what's *this?*"

"Insubordination."

"Do what they say," Officer Buck said, walking toward the truck.

"Now, that's better," Finch said.

He put the bill on Buck's cap back down.

Officer Billows was the first to climb into the van.

Trout put a folding chair by the bumper so the loading could be accomplished more quickly. But even with the chair Billows had a hard time. He grunted and groaned and rolled into the back of the truck and, in the light from the hallway he had just left, saw Sergeant House.

"They've got House," Billows said.

The light from the hallway reached only halfway into the van, so Billows moved slowly and carefully toward the big lump up front. "House," he said. "It's me, Billows. They've got us all."

Sergeant House was stretched out on his back. His limbs were arranged at odd angles. His right arm was underneath his back, and his left arm lay limp across his stomach. One leg was bent, the other was straight. Sergeant House's eyes were closed. His mouth was open.

Billows got down on his hands and knees so he could see better and crawled to within a couple of feet of his co-worker. He said over his shoulder, "Stay back, I think they've murdered House."

Billows crawled the rest of the way and loosened the top button on Sergeant House's shirt.

The two men were almost nose to nose when Sergeant House opened his eyes and said, "I'm alive, after all."

His body snapped back into shape.

Billows was on all fours and wanted to jump away, but he couldn't. All he could do was rear onto his knees. He couldn't stop rearing, though, and went over backwards onto his calves, which is hard on the thigh muscles. It stretches them and eventually pops them like rubber bands. As Billows reared backwards his feet shot out in front of him and the back of his skull hit the floor with a squishy thud.

"It serves him right," Sergeant House said, rising and dusting himself off. "Your practical joke almost gave me heart failure."

Lieutenant Bush was next into the van. He walked to where Billows lay stunned, and bent down to feel for a pulse. "I think he only knocked himself out," Lieutenant Bush said to the others.

"*Only?*" Heather wondered.

While the rest of the shift climbed solemnly into the truck, Lieutenant Bush got Billows by the shoulders and dragged him to a front corner, where he propped him up and tried his pulse again.

"Who thought up this practical joke?" Sergeant House asked.

"It's no joke." Lieutenant Bush put his ear to Billows's chest and said that the heartbeat was weak but steady.

"What do you *mean* this is no joke?"

"I guess they're kidnapping us."

Billows moved an arm and moaned. Lieutenant Bush told him he wasn't bleeding and he was okay.

Billows said feebly that he was most certainly *not* okay.

The others were told to sit along the sidewalls.

"Does anybody in here have a savings account at State National in Queens?" Sergeant House asked, trying to get a handle on what was going on.

"There's no bank called State National," Buck said.

"It's State some-goddamn-thing. Does anybody have an account at *any* bank in Queens?"

Nobody said anything.

When all the officers were seated, Trout climbed aboard with his flashlight and had everybody scoot together. He carried the flashlight in his left hand and the machine gun in his right.

42

"Do you have any idea where they're going to send us after they find out somebody *took* us?" Sergeant House said to Lieutenant Bush. "Do you have any idea what this is going to look like in the newspapers?"

"Be quiet and let me think."

"Think about a headline that says 'Police Snatched.' They'll send us to the Eighty-seventh, every last one of us. I know the deskman. You know what he's got in his desk? Not forms and pencils. *Flares.*"

"Let's hope," Heather said.

"Hope what?" Sergeant House asked.

"Hope we get transferred to somewhere like the Eighty-seventh."

"Why in God's name would anybody hope *that?*"

"It would mean we lived," Heather said.

The van fell silent.

Lieutenant Bush knew all about the Eighty-seventh Precinct. It was where, on a Saturday night, the police sometimes took to the holding cell.

Trout moved closer and told everybody to quit whispering.

His instructions were simple:

"Don't make a sound. Don't move. We'll open the back doors and check on you people from time to time. And you better be right where you are now."

"This man is hurt and needs medical attention," Lieutenant Bush said, pointing at Billows's skull.

"That's talk," Trout said.

The van fell silent again.

Trout hopped out.

Finch appeared at the back doors. "The rules established at the Geneva Convention don't apply here," he said, smiling wickedly.

He crawled underneath the truck, hopped into the cab, and moved the van away from the building.

Trout closed the back doors. He pulled down the handle

on the right door, fastening the two together. Then he jumped onto the rear bumper and used a key to lock the doors so they couldn't be opened from the inside.

They waited in the shadows behind the police station for about ten minutes, until the squad car driven by Officer Mounds arrived.

During a change in shifts a car or two or three or four, depending on the size and personality of the precinct, stays on duty so that a particularly violent area won't be completely without in-the-field protection, even for a few minutes. Because of the relative calm that prevailed within the confines of the Thirty-third Precinct on a drizzly weeknight, only one squad car fiddled around until the guard was changed.

Mounds drove around for twenty minutes every midweek night and, if nothing was going on, returned to the garage and filled out an overtime slip. Mounds was single and didn't mind the extra few minutes a night because they added up.

The money he earned covering the overlap period would help his heirs buy him a nice tombstone.

They got Mounds.

He pulled into the parking garage, yawned, and got out of his squad car. Two of them jumped out from behind a garbage bin and were on top of him before he could say "What is this, some kind of practical joke?"

"You're kidding," Mounds said instead when they grabbed him.

Mounds's reaction made Trout feel pretty confident about getting him into the truck without much trouble.

"This one is exactly my size," Finch said.

"Take your uniform off," Trout told Mounds.

"I knew it," Mounds said. "It's a practical joke."

They led Mounds, in his boxer shorts and T-shirt, to the truck and told him to get in.

"Hey," Mounds said when he saw his associates huddled together like rats.

"My God, they're still at it," Heather said.

Trout wanted to do something constructive in the six minutes they had to play with, so he took some crumpled notes from his jump-suit pocket and began reading from them.

"Go," Annabel said to the clock, which ticked forward to five minutes before midnight.

They were all by the front desk.

Trout went over the next part, about how he and Finch would set up near the museum and wait for the guards to go off duty. During that time Finch, dressed as a policeman, would handle any minor complaints that needed investigating.

"The guards won't change at the museum for at least a half hour," Trout said. "Sometimes it's forty minutes. Sometimes—"

"We all know what to do," Annabel said.

"We really do," Finch agreed, smiling. "All we have to do is stay alive until the end of this thing and go buy an island."

"How much do islands cost?" Roebuck wondered.

Finch told him you could get one with plumbing for half a million.

"No kidding," Roebuck said.

"Watch this," Annabel said.

She walked to Roebuck's desk.

"Can I help you, lady?" he asked.

"I've been mugged," Annabel said.

"Oh, Jesus Christ, how terrible."

Roebuck stood up and walked off the platform and gave Annabel a warm hug. "Why don't you have a seat over there and fill out some forms while I get you a nice pizza."

"See," Annabel said. "We're in perfect shape here."

Trout stuffed his notes into his pocket and walked toward the front door with his head down.

45

"Did I ever tell you about the time I was a bail bondsman when I was twenty-two?" Finch said.

He took his police revolver out of his holster and held it up to the light to admire it.

A bullet fell out of a chamber and bounced around on the wood floor.

Two

They met Lovely in a parking lot a mile from the Thirty-third Precinct. Lovely was in a van identical to the one that had been used at the police station. They had rented the vans for two days and had paid for them with cash.

Trout pulled the van full of police next to Lovely's truck, rolled down his passenger window, and asked how it was going.

Lovely yanked a handkerchief out of his pocket and mopped his round face. Although the night was cool, it was very humid, and Lovely was also nervous. "It's like a greenhouse in here," he said. "There's probably a tobacco plant growing in my shirt pocket from where my cigarettes spilled." It had been going okay in the parking lot, except for the times Lovely almost put his truck in gear and went home. "Listen, I don't know how to tell you this, but there's a police car behind you."

Trout leaned out his window and waved at Finch.

Finch waved his policeman's hat out his window.

"Is that who I think it is?" Lovely asked. "Don't answer that question. All I want to hear is directions."

That was the deal.

Lovely was Trout's neighbor; he was between engagements, and that was why he could use a thousand dollars. He had been engaged several times and owed one or two of these women some money. Consequently, he had agreed to do a little driving for Trout, but that was the extent of it. He would *not* do a little listening. If something went wrong and dogs came at them, he wanted to be able to tell the authorities that he had no idea what was going on. He wanted to take a lie detector test and pass. So far as Lovely was concerned, Trout was a fine, upstanding businessman; and there were vegetables in the back of the truck.

Finch pulled his police car in front of both vans, got out, and asked Lovely what was up.

"Go away," Lovely said.

"I can't. Didn't he tell you? We need to switch the bodies into your truck."

"One more joke like that and I quit," Lovely said. He didn't care a whole lot for Finch. He had played cards with him at Trout's, and once Finch put Scotch tape on his palm and stole seventy-five cents while pretending to call a quarter bet.

Trout got out of his truck and told Finch to get back in the police car and quit bothering Lovely. With Finch safely behind the wheel, Trout climbed into Lovely's truck, patted him on the knee, and told him that he was doing a great job. He then went over what was expected before the thousand dollars could change hands.

In a couple of minutes Trout was going to pull his truck out of the parking lot. Lovely would follow close behind. They would move to a spot approximately a mile away. There was

48

no need for a map. Lovely would maintain eye contact with Trout's truck all the way. If Trout made a light and Lovely got stuck, Trout would wait on the next block until his associate caught up.

"I'm no associate," Lovely said. "I'm a neighbor."

When Trout got to point A, he would pull to the right-hand curb and wave his hand out his window. This was where Lovely was to park his truck. It was by a Chinese restaurant, incidentally. Lovely would wait there awhile, roughly thirty to forty-five minutes, Trout guessed.

"I'll be parked on the block in front of you," Trout said.

Lovely was listening with his eyes closed.

After they had sat a block apart for anywhere from thirty minutes to an hour, Trout would again move his van forward. Lovely would again follow. They would move to point B and stop, and that would be it. Once Lovely had driven his truck to point B, Trout would give him an envelope containing one thousand dollars, and the remainder of Lovely's morning would be free.

Did Lovely have that?

"Go, stop, go," he said.

"Exactly," Trout agreed.

He told Lovely that if anything happened while he was parked by the Chinese restaurant, all he had to do was honk two longs and a short.

"We'll only be across an intersection from each other. Two longs and then a short. But don't honk for the hell of it. Don't honk unless something really serious happens."

Lovely opened his eyes.

"Something serious, like a flat tire."

Trout clasped Lovely by the shoulder and told him that although the trip from point A to point B might get a little hectic, there was absolutely no possibility of either injury or penalty.

49

"What do you mean *hectic?*"

"Bumpy. But remember, all you have to do for the thousand is exactly what I do. If I go over a curb, you go over a curb. You follow me. If I go through a fence, you go through a fence."

"I need some more money for curbs and fences. I need three hundred more, for a total of thirteen."

"It's done," Trout said.

Lovely squinted at Trout and said he wished he hadn't gotten the raise so quickly. "It means this is dangerous."

"All it means is you've got a generous neighbor."

Trout left Lovely sponging himself off.

"You steal from the Chinese, ten thousand of them will come after you," Lovely said, rolling his window up.

Trout wished Finch some good, quiet luck and said he would see him at the museum before too awfully long.

He got back into his truck and left the parking lot, going over a fair-sized curb.

Lovely honked two longs and a short.

"Yeah," Trout said, leaning out his window.

"Is this one of the curbs I was supposed to go over?" Lovely asked.

"No," Trout said.

"Right," Lovely said.

He left the parking lot using its driveway.

Annabel sat in the communications room at the Thirty-third Precinct and smoked.

She had taken a six-week course in computer operations and sincerely hoped that she had wasted Trout's tuition check.

There were six computers in the communications room.

Annabel sat with her nose a couple of feet from the computer linked to the 911-call network. The screen was blank. People were either behaving or a number of them had been beaten so severely, they couldn't get at a telephone.

Annabel familiarized herself with the various command buttons on the 911 computer and prayed for peace.

The 911 emergency-call system is truly amazing.

It works.

A 911 call goes to a central location, the main police headquarters where it is answered by a trained professional, not a telephone-company dropout. The 911 operators wear headphones and sit at computers. Incoming calls are rotated automatically from operator to operator so that one person won't handle ten straight catastrophies and become too nervous to handle the eleventh correctly.

Before a 911 call is activated into an operator's headset, a light flashes on his or her computer screen. The call clicks in after three or so seconds. This little bit of time gives the operator the opportunity to choke down a doughnut or swallow a cup of coffee.

When the 911 operator comes on, the caller should state his or her predicament simply and accurately.

It's frightening how many mistakes imperiled people make.

If somebody is trying to chop down your bedroom door with an axe, for example, you don't need to get too technical or mention how many hours this person has been lying drunk.

That wastes valuable seconds.

The most common mistake made by callers is when somebody says something like: "My husband is drunk and trying to murder me. Please come quick."

A lot of people forget to give their address.

You should state your address and name and then, if time permits, give a brief summary of what's left of your situation. After you've done that, you should remain on the line with the 911 operator because these people tape all conversations and make very good witnesses.

The point is: Keep talking.

Let the person who is trying to kill you know that you have informed an authority of his intent. More times than not, he will come to his senses and put the axe down. And in those other rare times, you will undoubtedly rest in peace, secure in the knowledge that whoever killed you will not be able to make up some lie about a prowler.

The 911 operator types your address, name, and the nature of your complaint into a computer. All calls are treated as genuine emergencies. It's the only way the system can work. The operators and officers get paid the same, whether the call is made by somebody in jeopardy or by a crank.

When you get right down to it, the police don't mind false alarms all that much.

It beats getting shot at.

Once a 911 operator has the pertinent information, he or she touches a button on the computer, and your emergency is routed to the appropriate precinct.

That takes about four seconds.

Each precinct has a special receiving computer for 911 calls. When a message is sent to a precinct, the communications officer touches a button to verify that the call has been received, and that's basically that.

The communications officer at the precinct gets the information from the computer and calls it to an officer in the field.

If you live in the Thirty-third Precinct, the best time to have somebody come through a bedroom door with an axe, that is, the best time in terms of having the call answered quickly and efficiently, is between 10 and 11 A.M. on a Tuesday. Everybody is fresh and alert after a dull Monday.

The worst time is after twelve on a wet weeknight.

True, there's not much traffic, but after midnight you don't get the cream of the crop. You get the old crows, the relatives of public officials, the rookies, or the imposters.

✿　✿　✿

George Johnson, who was drunk, hacked the last bit of bedroom door out of his way and looked at his wife, who held the telephone out in front of her at arm's length, as though it could stop somebody who weighed 210.

"That's no gun," he said, squinting.

"It's the police," Elizabeth Johnson said.

"Screw the police," George Johnson said. He reeled around and supported himself on a chest of drawers. He rested the blade of the axe on the floor.

"Did you hear that?" Elizabeth asked the 911 operator.

"We heard it," the operator said.

"I'll kill the police too."

"Did you hear *that?*"

"Yes."

"Well," George Johnson said of the fact that his wife had called the police on him. All he wanted to do was talk to her about a little matter that had been brought to his attention at the bar around the corner. One of George Johnson's acquaintances had seen Elizabeth rubbing a man's arm at lunch. And George Johnson simply wanted to discuss this matter with his wife, and then he wanted to chop her into small pieces and put her in a Baggie.

This marriage was not made in heaven.

It was an assembly-line job put together ten years ago in a marrying factory in Nevada.

"It was business," Elizabeth said of the lunch. The telephone was on her lap. She was a travel agent. "The man was sixty years old. We were putting together a tour."

"Of what, Holiday Inns?"

Elizabeth crossed her legs and told her husband he was going to feel like an idiot again in eight hours, so why didn't he go ahead and beg for her forgiveness now and get it over with so they wouldn't be late for work in the morning.

"Why," George asked, "would I feel like that?"

"Because you broke the door down."

53

"Oh, that won't make me feel bad. But this might."

George Johnson hoisted the axe over his head and chopped a little wood.

His wife screamed.

She had miscalculated his drunkenness and shouldn't have been so nonchalant.

George Johnson struck the chest of drawers such a mighty blow that the blade of the axe became deeply embedded in the top of the piece of furniture. He jerked on the handle, but nothing happened.

"Stay on the line," the 911 operator said. "Keep talking. Describe what's happening."

Okay, now he's . . ." Elizabeth said before the connection went dead.

Annabel blinked and jumped when one of her computers buzzed.

She put her cigarette aside and concentrated on the message that flashed onto her 911 screen. The first part read:

Domestic Disturbance

Annabel scooted her chair closer to the screen.

Man With Axe Threatening Wife

She read the last part from a distance of only nine or ten inches:

Complaint Suddenly Disconnected

"Hell," Annabel said.

She copied the address off the screen and wondered why in the world a person would try to chop up his wife on a worknight. Trout hadn't come across anything like *that* in all his research. All he'd come up with was loud radios.

Annabel acknowledged receipt of the 911 message, then she pushed a button on a box in front of her and established contact with Finch.

"David Three," she said.

This was the proper identification number for the police car Finch drove.

"What," he said quickly.

"Please call home."

"Okay."

What and *Okay* didn't remind Anabel of any program about law enforcement that she had ever seen on television.

Finch was sitting in a parking lot half a mile from the museum, beside a pay phone. After he received the request from Annabel, he got out of his squad car and called her back on one of the precinct's inside lines.

"Hi," he said.

"Yeah," Annabel said.

They didn't want to risk having an important message go out over the police radio. They might slip up with some of the terminology—all that ten-four and ten-twenty gibberish —and somebody might overhear them swearing at each other.

"So how's it going?" Finch asked. "It's too damp even for the rats out here."

"Be quiet," Annabel told him. "Something just came in on the nine-one-one computer."

"Hang on while I get a pencil and paper."

"There's a man with an axe going at his wife."

Finch stopped digging through his pockets. "I shouldn't have any trouble remembering that."

Annabel read the address and apartment number.

Finch wanted to know exactly what in the hell was going on here.

"Listen, Finch. Try to stop them from killing each other. But if they won't, bring somebody on down here. Only as a last resort, though."

"I know what to do," Finch said.

"If you can't break it up, *let* them kill each other."

"I'm not carrying around any chunks of people in the trunk, I'll tell you that for sure."

Annabel told Finch to call her back after he finished his investigation.

"All Trout mentioned for this time of night was a fender bender or a dogfight or something like that."

"I only work here," Annabel said, hanging up.

Annabel started a new cigarette from the stub of one still burning, coughed, and dialed the Ross Detective Agency. She spoke with Ross himself, who was either eating a sandwich or being strangled. Annabel guessed that he was being choked to death by an irate customer.

The only case Ross could solve had cheap wine in it.

"Yes, hello, what is it you want?" he said.

Trout wanted somebody standing by in case two or more emergencies occurred at the same time—before he could get into the museum. That made sense to Annabel. She just didn't know why it had to be Ross, who had asked to see her knees the only time she had met him.

"It's me," Annabel said into her telephone, "Annabel."

"I don't know anybody by that name," Ross said.

"Listen, goddamn it."

"Oh, yeah, hang on. I do know one. The one with Trout that cusses like a sailor."

Annabel reluctantly told Ross it was time for him and his people to stand by.

Ross said, "You got it."

He informed Annabel that as they spoke two of his most trusted employees were at his side. Furthermore, one was wearing an authentic police uniform that rented for sixty dollars from a costume shop over near Broadway.

Trout's contingency plan called for one or more of Ross's butchers to impersonate policemen in the event that Finch was busy. Or dead. Annabel told Ross that if an emergency arose in the next few minutes, she would call back and state the nature of the problem, and the address.

"Tell Don here," Ross said.

"It's me," Don said, coming onto the line.

"Do you understand what you're supposed to do if I call back?"

"Sure, play like a cop."

"One of you is supposed to pretend to be a uniformed officer. Another is to be a detective. You won't be going anywhere in a police car. You'll be arriving in a plain car. One in a suit, one in a uniform, do you understand that?"

"A moron could understand that," Don said. "What kind of suit?"

"A business suit. If you're needed, all you do is take names and break up whatever is happening. Then leave."

"Anybody could understand that."

Ross came back on the line and said it looked to him like Trout was finally onto something really big and that the agency should perhaps share in a percentage of the take. He said that he had his best men on this project, not the vo-tech dropouts. The very least he wanted was a hundred dollars for extra insurance in case one of his all-stars got blasted.

Annabel read Ross her MasterCard number for the extra insurance, then slammed the phone down.

Mercifully there was nothing else on any of the computers, so she rang Roebuck at the front desk. She informed him about the problem with the axe and asked how it was going down there.

"Great," Roebuck said. "This one old foreigner comes in about two minutes ago, waving his arms and mumbling about something or other. I couldn't understand a thing he said, so I gave him a map of the city."

"What'd he do?"

"He put it in his pocket and left."

"Good work, Roebuck."

"Thanks a lot."

She hung up and tried to think of a pleasant way to inform Trout about Finch's bad luck.

"Hi, guess what?" was about the best she could do.

When the pay phone next to Trout rang, he got out and answered it, still keeping an eye on the museum two blocks up the road. The street he was on dead-ended at the museum's front gates.

Although it was still moist outside, Trout was in a position to see headlights when the guards going off duty left the museum property.

Trout couldn't *guess what* and was in no mood to try, because Lovely was back there sticking his head out his window every minute.

"I just sent Finch to an apartment where a man was taking an axe to his wife."

Trout said nothing.

"Allegedly, of course."

"Well, for God's sake," Trout finally said.

"Ross has been notified. One *thinks.* I called him and told him to stay by the phone, but those people are a little stupid."

"Well, for God's sake," Trout said again, looking back at Lovely.

"So," Annabel said. "I guess what I'll do next is send you the all-clear after Finch checks back in, or notify his next of kin."

"Turn your goddamn lights off," Trout said loudly.

"What?" Annabel asked.

"Nothing. Listen, Finch can handle it. If you get another emergency, call me back. Let's stay away from Ross as long as we can. I'll go answer the next complaint myself."

"You'll answer an emergency *in the van?*"

"If there is one. There shouldn't be at this hour."

58

"You haven't even got a uniform."

"Listen, goddamn it."

"Don't you goddamn me," Annabel said.

"Good-bye."

"Good-bye."

Trout slammed the receiver in place and trotted back to Lovely's truck. During the jog, which was no more than a hundred yards, Trout didn't see anybody. He attempted to open Lovely's passenger door, but it was locked.

Trout banged on the window.

Lovely rolled it down.

He looked as though he had just stepped out of a shower. He was soaked.

"Your headlights are on," Trout said.

"You're kidding." Lovely reached up and turned them off and said he must have got the knob for the lights confused with the cigarette lighter.

"You don't need to keep sticking your head out the window."

"It's hot in here. It's ninety degrees at least."

Trout leaned inside and picked a paper bag off the front seat. He wadded it up and stuffed it into his pocket and cautioned Lovely against leaving anything in the cab. "They charge extra if they have to vacuum the truck when we take it back."

"I don't believe that for a second," Lovely said.

Trout patted Lovely on the arm and left his neighbor sitting in a pool of panic.

"Hey, Trout," Lovely half shouted after him.

Trout walked back and said he would appreciate it if Lovely didn't yell out his name in public.

"Why not?"

"Just humor me."

"I couldn't humor an infant."

"What is it you want?"

59

"There's something in the back of your truck, right?"
Trout nodded.
"Answer this one question. Is it animal or mineral?"
"Animal."
"It's mink coats. I knew it was mink coats all along."
"Right. We stole them at noon, but they were the wrong size and we're taking them back."
Lovely sniffed and said nothing.
Trout turned and went back to his truck.
When Trout had crossed the intersection, Lovely reached into the inside pocket of his windbreaker and removed a pint of cherry vodka. He had a sip. It tasted fair. Too much, though, turned a man's stomach into the Red Sea.
Lovely watched as Trout stopped at the back of his truck and listened at the doors. Lovely had another sip and wondered what he had ever done to deserve this; he had never killed anybody.

You could have heard a pin drop in the back of Trout's truck.
A bowling pin.
Maybe.
Sergeant House was making everybody mad by demanding to know precisely how much each of them had in the bank. He was convinced that they were being held for ransom and that the kidnappings could be traced back to the savings and loan company where he had hidden his money.
Billows was feeling well enough to nod slightly.
Mounds, who was in his underwear, was the only person who didn't mind discussing his personal finances.
"Nine hundred dollars," Mounds said.
"What do you *mean* nine hundred dollars?" Sergeant House asked incredulously.
"I *mean*, I have nine hundred dollars in the bank."

"What the hell do you eat, dog food?"

"I live flashy," Mounds answered.

"Why," Sergeant House asked around, "would they kidnap somebody for nine hundred dollars?"

"Maybe," Heather guessed, "they're going to kill us all to disguise the motive. Maybe they really want to kill *one* of us."

Lieutenant Bush stood in the middle of the truck and asked for some quiet. Now that they had been driven away from the precinct, it was going to be very difficult to hide from the press and their superiors the fact that they had been taken. If, for example, they were released in downtown Omaha, there was going to be some powerful explaining to do. If they were being held for ransom, it would be the lead story, naturally.

"We need to get out of here," Lieutenant Bush said.

This proclamation was greeted with several profanities.

"The reason they have us isn't important."

"It's pretty important if Heather is right and we're going to be murdered," somebody said.

A few others agreed with that line of thought.

Officer Buck said, "We kick the doors open and maul them."

"This door is pretty heavy," somebody said.

"If we don't knock the door out on the first try," Mounds said, "we're in big trouble. They'll hear the racket and come and get us. Still, it's probably worth a try."

"It's nonsense," Sergeant House said. "Mounds is for it because he has nothing to lose. Bag ladies have more than nine hundred dollars in the bank."

"I drive a Lincoln Continental, for your information," Mounds said.

"Whose is it?" Sergeant House asked.

"Knock it off." Lieutenant Bush stomped his foot a few

times. "How about this? We could all line up on one side of the truck and throw our shoulders against the opposite wall and try to knock the van over onto its side."

"Are you serious?" somebody from up near the front asked.

Another officer said this wasn't the kind of idea you kicked around. It was the kind you trampled to death.

"The only way out of here is headfirst," Buck said.

It was at this point in the discussion, as Buck was yelling at Lieutenant Bush and Billows was trying to locate Sergeant House so he could punch him in the face, that Trout opened the doors and shined a flashlight inside. The officers from the Thirty-third Precinct shielded their eyes from the light and backed away from the doors.

"What's going on in here?" Trout asked.

"Nothing important," Lieutenant Bush answered. "We were just stretching."

Trout asked what he had to do—shoot somebody?

He took his machine gun from the gunnysack and banged the butt against the floor of the truck. He said that if he heard one more sound, one cough, one anything, he was going to return and restore order *permanently.*

He closed and locked the doors with the key and got back behind the wheel.

After a few seconds Lieutenant Bush and Officer Buck crawled to the center of the van and whispered back and forth into each other's ear. Their plan was, in turn, whispered to the rest of the group.

Attempting to bust out was now a very low percentage play.

The only chance they had was to remain extremely quiet and attempt to disarm their captor the next time he checked on their well-being. He had appeared extremely dangerous this last time. In the glow of his flashlight he appeared very nearly wild. He had seriously frightened them.

So what the officers in the back of the truck were going

62

to do was try to put somebody in a position to suddenly overwhelm whoever opened the doors next.

That somebody was Buck.

They would attempt to arrange a sling over the doors. This sling would hang from hinges. Buck would suspend himself up by the ceiling, and when the doors were opened again, he would reach down and break the neck of, or at least knock unconscious, one of the bastards who had stolen them.

"Everybody give me your shirts and belts," Buck whispered.

"Yeah, sure," Heather said.

Finch pulled his police car to the curb in front of the apartment building where, four stories up, a man named George Johnson had last been heard going berserk. Finch turned off his flashing light, got out, and looked up into the mist, more or less expecting to see somebody or something fly out a window.

The apartment building was average, which meant that a person could put his name on a waiting list and three years later pick up a tidy little efficiency with a walk-in bedroom and lean-in closets for eight hundred, plus bills.

There was no doorman out front. There were some large black men huddled together under an awning looking *very* suspicious.

Finch released the strap that held his weapon in his holster, locked the squad car, squared his shoulders, and walked purposefully toward the entrance.

When he was six feet away from the four men, he looked at their clothes for bloodstains and wondered if one of them was the suspect.

Everybody nodded at each other.

After an uncomfortable silence the largest man standing under the awning stepped forward and extended his hand.

"I be black," this man said.

63

Finch, who thought that displaying pride in one's heritage was a fine thing, licked his lips and shook the man's hand.

"I be the police," Finch said, reducing the possible communications gap to its lowest common denominator.

The four black men frowned.

"What did you say?" one of them asked Finch.

"I said, I be the police."

"Why'd you say that?"

Finch adjusted his hat. "Because it's the truth. Listen, I have to go."

The man who had spoken first stood to his full height, which Finch guessed was about six-four. He wore a cashmere coat. He showed Finch his hands. He slowly opened his cashmere coat and then, under that, his suit coat. He carefully removed from an inside pocket a billfold made of eel, which was very big this year.

Finch didn't know what was going on.

He didn't particularly want to either.

Finch smiled at the billfold and said he had almost got some eel cowboy boots not long ago but had worried about how they would do in bad weather. "The eels seem to do okay in the water, though, don't they?"

Finch smiled.

Nobody else did.

The man in the cashmere coat sorted through some business and credit cards. He selected a business card and handed it to Finch, who accepted and read it. The letters were raised gold.

The card said:

Dr. I. B. Blaque.

Under that was:

Physician.

And then below were a couple of addresses and telephone numbers and even a telex listing.

"My mistake," Finch said.

64

He shook his head and handed the card back to Dr. Blaque and apologized for the misunderstanding with the language.

"You are contemptible," Dr. Blaque said slowly and with perfect enunciation. "You are a disgrace to your uniform. People like you cause race riots."

The other three men nodded and looked even bigger.

"It's all that television where everybody talks funny," Finch said.

The physician took a step forward.

"Don't make me run you in," Finch said, placing his hand on his gun butt. "Or shoot you."

Dr. Blaque put his billfold back into his pocket and buttoned his cashmere coat. "You'll regret this Mounds," he said.

Finch looked down at Mounds's name tag and felt a little better.

"By this time tomorrow you'll be walking a beat in the most dangerous alleys in this city. You're going to be checking abandoned buildings for drug dealers."

"He knows the mayor," one of the men said. "They've had dinner together."

"He could have your badge for this," another of them agreed.

Dr. Blaque copied Finch's badge and squad-car numbers on the back of a business card, and then the four men walked off into the night.

Your mayor's moustache, Finch thought.

Finch entered the outer lobby and buzzed the Johnson apartment on the intercom. There was no answer. Finch thought that might be a good sign. Maybe no one was home. Or, nobody was alive.

Finch hung up and searched the apartment directory for a manager listing.

"Wonderful," he said.

65

There was no such listing.

He buzzed at random someone from the middle of the second row of tenants and kept his finger on the button.

Eventually somebody who sounded sleepy said, "What is it?"

"This is the police," Finch said. "Hit the door buzzer. I need to get into this building to check out a complaint."

"You addicts don't have much imagination," the person at the other end said, and hung up.

"But . . . " Finch said.

He picked another tenant and tried again. This time the buzzer was answered much more quickly.

"This is the police," Finch said. "Let me in."

"Sure thing," the person at the other end said quickly and pleasantly.

Finch blinked.

The door buzzed.

Finch opened the door and stuck his foot inside.

"You get it?" the man at the other end asked.

"Yeah," Finch said. "Listen."

The door stopped buzzing.

"You hadn't ought to do this kind of thing so fast. I could have been trying to gain entry under false pretenses."

The man at the other end laughed and said that in these hard times everybody had to stick together—everything being the poor people who had some spunk and were not afraid to try something that could blow up in their faces.

Finch frowned.

"Now wait just a minute," he said. "You're a damn *criminal*, aren't you? You're up there going through somebody's apartment."

"That's no way to talk to the FBI," the man said.

He laughed and hung up.

Finch also hung up and entered the lobby.

❖　❖　❖

Finch took the elevator to the fourth floor and peeked out. The hallway was dim and quiet.

"Police," Finch said quietly.

He took a scrap of paper out of his pocket and jammed it into a hole in front of the electric eye so that the elevator would remain on the fourth floor in case there was a shoot-out and he had to make a quick retreat.

In front of the elevator was a sign indicating apartments A through K were to the left.

Finch took his revolver from its holster and moved reluctantly in that direction.

The doors in this building didn't quite fit the frames.

Most of them stopped an inch or so before they got to the floor.

Finch tiptoed to the Johnsons' door, got down on his hands and knees, and determined that at least the area just inside the apartment was dark.

"Collecting for the paper," Finch said softly.

There was no response.

Finch got back up and placed his left hand on the doorknob, wishing with all his might that the apartment would be locked or that furniture would be piled against the door so he wouldn't have to go inside.

But the door wasn't locked.

It wasn't even chained.

The hinges didn't even squeak.

The door swung open into darkness, which made Finch nervous. Standing there against the light from the hallway made him an easy target.

So he stepped inside quickly and closed the door.

He put his pistol back in its holster and unhooked a flashlight from a hoop on his belt. He put a hand over the end of the flashlight so the room wouldn't suddenly be flooded with light, making him a sitting duck once more.

Finch determined from the slabs of light that he was in

67

the living room, and that nothing there was out of the ordinary.

"Maintenance," Finch said.

He took his left hand from in front of the flashlight, which he now shined around the living room. From where he stood he could see the kitchen off to the right and the entrance to what was probably the bedroom to the left.

It didn't take a genius to figure out what had happened —a genius or a real police officer. The bedroom had been the scene of the crime. The perpetrator had fled, obviously. Otherwise, Finch would already have been engaged in hand-to-hand combat.

Finch was beginning to feel a lot better about this investigation.

Everything was so quiet.

Had a murderer still been inside the apartment, Finch would have had to do something, like issue him a warning. This way, all he had to do was check out the bedroom and then use the telephone in the kitchen to inform Annabel that all was well, and that he was ready to support Trout at the museum.

It was probably wishful thinking, but maybe the person who called in the complaint had merely been knocked out and was right now lying peacefully on the bed.

With this positive thought in mind Finch opened the bedroom door and turned on the overhead light, which was bright.

They were making love under a sheet.

Finch wasn't sure what they were doing until the man threw his part of the sheet off and roared.

"Oh, no," Finch said.

"I *knew* it," the man said to his wife. He was obviously

still a little drunk. He was having trouble maintaining his balance, even though he was only sitting up in bed. His eyes were almost puffed, or fatted, shut.

"It's only the police I called earlier, remember?" the woman said. "Before you ripped the phone out."

She grabbed the sheet and held it up to her chin.

George Johnson rolled off the bed away from Finch. He landed with a loud thump and crawled for a closet.

Elizabeth said to Finch, "He thinks we're lovers. He thinks I'm a nymphomaniac. He's getting his gun."

"This woman is no nymphomaniac," Finch said, pointing at her.

Finch's hopeless tone seemed to give George Johnson strength and confidence. He got to his feet and began grabbing at the closet doors, which were a little stuck. Finch had never seen anything like it. George Johnson looked like a rhino that had been shot with a tranquilizer dart. He was lunging and taking swipes at anything within reach.

Elizabeth got out of bed and wrapped the sheet around her.

George Johnson got one of the closet doors open and ripped it from its grooves. Smiling, he threw it onto the bed. He charged into the closet, flinging hangers out behind him. He backed out seconds later with a shotgun in one hand and a box of shells in the other.

Elizabeth ran by Finch.

"Somebody stop," Finch said.

He watched George Johnson stab some shells at the shotgun, and then he turned and ran too.

There was an explosion in the bedroom, and part of a wall behind Finch disintegrated.

Finch ran from the Johnsons' apartment—it sure didn't look like they'd be getting their deposit back—into the hall.

The elevator was still waiting, but heading that way was out of the question. If the elevator didn't close quickly with Finch inside, the naked man with the shotgun would have a relatively simple shot.

Finch sprinted for the Exit sign at the end of the hallway. He had to run some fifty yards and he smashed into the door with his shoulder, which hurt. He ran down the stairs two or three at a clip and had established a comfortable rhythm by the time he got to the second-floor landing, where he passed Elizabeth Johnson, who was having to go slowly because of the length of the sheet she wore.

"Take me to my sister's," she called out as Finch jumped by.

"You better hurry," he said over his shoulder.

Finch found a yellow slicker in the trunk of his squad car, and he turned his back politely as Elizabeth Johnson wrestled into it.

"Thanks for not shooting him," she said, wiggling into the front seat.

"I'll come back after he gets the inheritance and shoot him then," Finch said. "Who is it, an uncle?"

"His grandmother. How'd you know about that?"

Finch couldn't think of another reason why anybody would live in the same cage with a person like that. "I'll say one thing, you people certainly know how to kiss and make up."

"It's a job," Elizabeth Johnson said.

Her sister lived only a few miles away. Finch made the trip in five minutes and was thanked for his help, even though he should have spoken up about being in the apartment.

The slicker didn't cover much of Elizabeth Johnson's legs, so she tied the sheet around her waist and said she'd bring the yellow jacket right back.

70

"Throw it out the window," Finch said.

He left before she did.

While Trout was sitting calmly in his moving van waiting for the all-clear signal, and while Finch was trying to pull himself together after having been shot at by a naked man, and while Annabel was watching the computers and holding her breath:

Roebuck was getting mad.

A woman and her son were standing in front of his desk, bitching.

Four other woman were sitting in folding chairs off to Roebuck's left. Two men were with these four women, helping complete the forms Roebuck had handed out. Three of these women—the one standing by the desk and two of those seated—had just had their purses swiped. The eight people had swirled in through the front door moments before, demanding justice.

There had been a party in a building a block and a half south, and as three or four couples left the building two men jumped out of the shadows to relieve the obviously well-off women of their handbags. The thieves wore masks, and one of them limped and the other had an accent, or something like that.

When the eight people entered the Thirty-third Precinct, they all talked at once.

Roebuck told them to relax and was now getting to the heart of the matter.

"I want to see the hands of everybody who had a purse stolen," he said, shuffling forms and pencils. It was damn confusing, what with all the witnesses who had accompanied the victims.

"My mother had her purse stolen," the young man standing in front of Roebuck said. "We've told you that six times."

This person's hair was slicked back and he wore wire-rimmed glasses. He looked like a character out of the twenties and was too prissy, in Roebuck's opinion.

"You live with your mother, do you?" Roebuck said, studying a form.

"That's right."

"Charles Emerson."

"Must we continue to repeat the incidentals?"

"I used to live with my mother," Roebuck said. "Then I turned eighteen."

He looked around Mrs. Emerson and her son at the hands that were being raised by the other victims, who sat in the folding chairs along the wall. Two women and one man had hands in the air.

"*You* lost a purse?" Roebuck said to the man, who was wearing a greenish tuxedo.

"My wife. After her purse was grabbed, she became ill."

"Oh," Roebuck said, scratching his chin. "Then go ahead and fill a form out."

"Do I list my birth date or my wife's?"

"Which form have you got?"

"The victim's," the man in the tux said.

"Both," Roebuck told him.

"There's no room in the box."

"Write on the back."

"I guess you might as well do what he says, Mother," Charles Emerson said of the form she was holding as though it might bite her. She accepted a pencil from Roebuck and sat down beside her friends to work on her statement.

Charles Emerson had already completed his report.

Roebuck glanced at it.

"It says under 'Occupation' that you're your mother's manager. What is she, a singer?"

Charles Emerson folded his arms. "An investor."

"That must be pretty tough work for the both of you."

Charles Emerson shook his head and removed a small tape recorder from his briefcase, which was leather and which he must have stuck under his coat during the crime. He ran the recorder back some, then flipped a switch to Record. "What happens now?"

Roebuck looked at the tape recorder out of the corner of his eye, as though it were some kind of insect. He sat very still. He was going to lull it to sleep and then reach out with a meaty fist and smash it.

"When?" Roebuck asked.

"This minute."

Still looking at the tape recorder, Roebuck said, "I collect the forms. You go home. We'll look for your purses and call you tomorrow."

"It only happened," Charles Emerson said, looking at his watch, which was a Rolex, *"eight minutes ago."*

"What's this thing doing on?" Roebuck asked of the tape recorder.

"I'm documenting this discussion. Several members of our group had a great deal of money and other valuables in their purses, not to mention items of tremendous sentimental value. We're not entirely pleased with the way this investigation is being handled."

"What investigation?"

"Several of us believe that something should be done *now,* that some type of recovery mechanism should be triggered, instead of wasting all this time on paperwork."

"So this thing is just on for the hell of it, or what?"

Roebuck moved his right hand nearer the tape recorder.

"It's on," Charles Emerson said, his voice heavy with exasperation, "in case there are legal repercussions."

What Roebuck wanted to do then was rise from his cheap chair, lean forward, and drive Charles Emerson into the ground. He could use some manners. Roebuck could have been, after all, a hard working Joe trying to earn an honest buck. This was no way to treat a man in blue, had Roebuck really been one. But Roebuck remembered what Trout said about punching people, so instead of pretending that the tape recorder was a paycheck and that Charles Emerson's mouth was a night-deposit slot, Roebuck took a deep breath and said with his mouth no more than six inches from the recorder, "Fill the forms out is the way it works."

"Excuse me," Charles Emerson said. He whirled around and rejoined his friends and loved ones.

When Charles Emerson was out of range, Roebuck picked up the tape recorder and said into it:

"This is pissing me off."

After a brief conference *all eight* of them approached Roebuck's desk and stood in a neat row in front of it.

Roebuck collected the forms and put them in two stacks, Victims on the left and Witnesses on the right.

"We have decided," Charles Emerson said, speaking for the group, "not to go home. We have decided to communicate further with a person in a position of responsibility. We realize that the hour is late, but we simply can't let this matter go unresolved."

"You can probably sleep in tomorrow morning," Roebuck said.

"So will you please call your superior?"

Roebuck looked over his shoulder at the clock. It was twenty or so before one. "My superior."

"Please."

"Have some seats over there."

"Thank you very much," Charles Emerson said. He led his group back to the ratty chairs. They all sat down and crossed their legs and stared at Desk Officer Roebuck, who picked up the telephone and wondered what he was going to do next.

He said, "It's busy. My superior is busy."

"We'll wait," Charles Emerson said.

"You'll wait."

Roebuck looked at the Victims' forms. He got a pencil and a note pad and added up how much they had lost. He wrote this figure on a piece of paper and tore it from the note pad and stuffed it in his shirt pocket. "I'll be right back," he said. "I'm going to check on my superior and a couple of other things."

Roebuck was doing his best to improvise a solution to this god-awful mess. Trout had trusted him to handle the important position of desk officer, and Roebuck was going to give it his all-time best shot.

Charles Emerson nodded his thanks for the cooperation.

Roebuck wondered what Charles Emerson had done while the thugs took his mother's purse, other than have palpitations.

Roebuck went down the stairs to the rest room. He went to the sink and emptied his pockets and put the contents on a shelf below the mirror. He took the cash out of his billfold and added everything up. It came to $105.75. He wrapped the $105.75 in a paper towel, turned the light off, and trudged back upstairs to his desk.

"My superior is still busy," he said. "But I stopped by the property room and I might have a little good news. We found one of your purses, a black one. Here's this."

Roebuck emptied the $105.75 onto his desk. His plan was for the victims to split the cash and go home and leave him the hell alone.

Charles Emerson walked to Roebuck's desk and looked distastefully at the money, most of which was badly wrinkled. "My mother lost seven and a quarter."

"So it wasn't her purse we found. You're lucky to get *anything* back, friend. You don't know how lucky you are."

75

"Did anybody lose some soiled money?" Charles Emerson asked his group.

That was a silly question.

"Maybe whoever stole it wrinkled it," Roebuck suggested.

"I believe you have recovered somebody else's purse."

"Are you going to take this or not?"

"Of course not," Charles Emerson said. "We're going to sit and wait."

"You don't have insurance?"

"That's not the point."

"What is the point?"

"Peace of mind," Charles Emerson said.

Roebuck put the money back in his pocket.

Finch was in a terrible mood too.

He had just tried some positive thinking. He tried to replace the memory of the shotgun blast with something that happened when he was twelve—when he knocked in the winning run for his peewee baseball team—but it didn't work worth a damn. All Finch could think of was the ugly naked man trying to kill him.

He parked directly in front of the main doors at the Thirty-third Precinct and stomped inside and, before he knew it, was surrounded by people in formal evening clothes.

"We've been robbed," one of them said.

Finch stretched himself onto his toes and looked at Roebuck, who was grinning and waving from his desk.

"What the hell is going on here?" Finch yelled at Roebuck.

"It's a convention," he called back, "of victims."

"Thank *God*," Charles Emerson said, identifying himself. He shook Finch's cold, damp hand.

Finch again asked what was going on.

"We've been robbed."

"Who did it?" Finch asked, half expecting one of the people to point at Roebuck.

"Two men," Charles Emerson answered. "Thugs."

"Give me some air here."

The people in the long dresses and shiny suits gave Finch some breathing and thinking room.

"Now that you're here, I'm going on a coffee break," Roebuck said.

Finch told the people who had been robbed to please sit back down, and he walked to the front desk. He took his hat off and brought Roebuck up to date on how he had walked in on two people who were making love, and been shot at like a goddamn jackrabbit. He had lost his pistol running down the stairs and had come to get a fresh weapon and to tell Annabel he was still alive.

"I would have traded places with you in a second," Roebuck said.

Roebuck brought Finch up to date: These people had some purses snatched and were unwilling simply to fill out a form and beat it. They wanted dialog with a person in charge. They wanted to see their tax dollars at work. They wanted peace of mind.

"Terrific," Finch said. He put his hat on and walked over to the eight people, all of whom were smiling brightly because they were certain that the field officer would restore order to this unpleasant situation.

Roebuck followed along, carrying the tape recorder.

"Here is the way it works," Finch said, stuffing his hands into his pockets. "There's a pecking order, when it comes to crime."

Most of the eight people nodded.

Very good, Roebuck thought.

"Murder is at the top of the list. When we get a situation where somebody has been stabbed, has had their guts ripped out like a fish, what we do is pursue this event with reckless determination."

Finch made a motion as if he were ripping out somebody's guts; it was not a pretty sight. "Murder takes priority over everything else."

Everybody nodded some more.

"Then there's rape, hostage situations, bombings, armed robbery, gang fights, all the way down to purse snatchings. Purse snatching is at the bottom of the barrel. We can't take a person off a murder and put him on a purse. Sorry, but that's the way it is. We've got descriptions of the two men who robbed you. When some more people come on duty in the morning, we'll get right on it."

Roebuck patted Finch on the back and said, "Nice going."

Charles Emerson considered Finch's statement and rejected the proposed course of action.

"You *what?*" Finch asked.

"He's the one that's been causing all the trouble," Roebuck whispered.

Finch nodded and squinted.

"We demand immediate action," Charles Emerson said, as though his opinion mattered. "The people who took our purses had knives. It was not a simple mugging. This was attempted murder."

"*Please* go home," Finch said.

"No," Charles Emerson said. "I'll have *everybody's* badge over this incident if the need arises."

"That's the last goddamn time I want to hear *that* tonight," Finch said, drawing Roebuck's revolver from its holster. "I mean, this morning. Put your hands up."

Finch waved the gun at the eight people seated along the wall.

Even Roebuck was startled by Finch's unexpected mid-course correction. He recovered quickly, however, and told Finch not to shoot them in the lobby, in case somebody else came in with a complaint. "It would make a mess."

One of the women opened her mouth to scream.

Finch pointed the gun in her direction.

The woman closed her mouth.

"Frisk them," Finch said.

"I think somebody already did that," Roebuck said sheepishly. "Remember, when they were robbed."

"The men."

Roebuck had the men empty their pockets.

Charles Emerson raised his hand.

"Ask your question quietly," Finch said.

"What is the meaning of this?"

"You're under arrest."

"*Why?*"

"Loitering," Finch said.

He had everybody get up, and he marched them single file toward the stairs.

"Here, you forgot this," Roebuck said, tossing Charles Emerson his tape recorder.

Finch guided the Charles Emerson party downstairs to the holding cell, which looked dark and moist and depressing, even from the outside.

"Do you have any blankets?" one of the women asked.

Finch told them to sit quietly on the benches inside the cell. By *quietly* he meant breathlessly. One of the women hiked her gown above her knees, sat on a rickety bench, and held in a sob.

Finch closed the door on the holding cell and headed back toward the stairs.

"I didn't know you could loiter *in* a police station," Charles Emerson said weakly.

Finch turned the light off.

"It's a new law aimed at people who keep confessing to crimes they didn't do," he said.

He stepped into the hallway and listened.

"The man is sick," Charles Emerson said.

"Be quiet or he might come back and spray something on us," someone else guessed.

"I hope it's pine air freshener," a woman said.

Finch left them quietly arguing about what to put in the lawsuit.

When Trout originally drew this particular scene on the blackboard, he certainly hadn't colored in enough circles to represent the spectators.

"God only knows who else could come in through the front door," Roebuck said. "What if eight more come in, and eight more?"

Annabel poured him some coffee.

They were visiting by the front desk.

"I'm not going to any more domestic disturbances," Finch said.

"The computers are clear," Annabel assured him.

"They better stay that way," Finch told her.

"Hell, I haven't even got a gun," Roebuck said.

Annabel was not in very good shape either. There was one computer up there that beeped every few seconds. This computer showed what was going on all over the city. About ten minutes ago a gang fight had moved to within half a block of the easternmost border of the Thirty-third Precinct before it was broken up. As Annabel tracked the gang fight she smoked six cigarettes.

"You can use mine," Annabel said, handing Roebuck her gun, which was a small one.

"What is it, a water gun?" Finch wondered.

Roebuck put the tiny thing in his holster, and it slipped

through and fell to the floor. He picked it up and put it in his front shirt pocket. You couldn't even see part of it sticking out.

Annabel said that she should get back to the communications room.

Roebuck got some fresh forms out of the top drawer.

Finch put his hat back on. "Give me ten minutes to get into position before you send Trout the all-clear."

"Maybe it's downhill from here," Roebuck said as Finch walked toward the front door.

"Hell is, that's for sure," Finch said over his shoulder. "It's downhill from here. About six feet downhill."

A couple of the intangibles Trout had worried so much about finally caught up with him.

The intangibles had been watching from the shadows for fifteen minutes, plotting strategy.

They were hung up on which window to smash in.

They stood in puddles of water and wondered once again if they were being set up, because this looked too simple, and they also wondered if a gun butt would knock the window out with one blow. They wondered further if the passenger window was the most logical side to go for.

One of them loved it and had been ready to take a flying leap since the second they arrived.

The other one only *liked* it and wanted everything down pat.

"You know the main thing I don't like?" the one who only liked it said. "It's that neither of us has been living right. People who don't live right don't usually get the breaks."

The one who loved it said that was a really dumb thing to say. If they *had* been living right, they wouldn't even be considering something like this. They'd be home in bed in suburbia, or at church. "We smash in both windows at once, and that's all there is to it."

"I haven't got a gun," the one who kind of liked it said.

"Use your head," the one who loved it said.

"Are you crazy? That would hurt."

"I meant pick up that damn rock over there."

Trout was thinking ahead to the museum when a man with a long forehead yanked the driver's door open and stuck a pistol in his ribs.

"Be quiet," the man said. His face had several scars on it.

An instant later the passenger door was yanked open by a man carrying a rock. "Thanks for not locking the doors," this one said. "Not that it would have mattered. If they had been locked, we would have smashed them in."

"Scoot over," the one poking a gun into Trout's midsection said.

Trout couldn't think of anything to say except "Don't do this." He felt slightly sick. He couldn't *believe* he hadn't locked the doors. This was not the kind of unexpected challenge he assumed they would have to overcome. This was *dangerous*. "Don't do this under any circumstance," he said sincerely.

The two men were not impressed with Trout's presentation.

"We don't particularly want to have to shoot you," the man with the gun said.

"But we will," the other one added, smiling. "It's this damn unemployment. It makes you crazy. Nobody we rob has got any money."

Trout looked from the man on his left to the man on his right. They were awful looking. They were unshaven. Their clothing was hardly more than rags. How could people like this be permitted to walk the streets? Not tonight, necessarily, when there were no police. But they should have been picked up *long* ago.

Trout had no choice except to scoot over into the middle of the front seat.

He was joined in the cab of the truck by a man named Pike, who had the scars and who had loved going after the truck from the first, and by a man named Suggs, who wore a crew cut and who felt a lot better about things already.

"I love it now," Suggs said.

Pike got in behind the wheel and closed the door and moved the steering wheel left and right and familiarized himself with the rather complicated control panel.

"This is one nice truck," he said.

"Yeah," Suggs agreed. "It's got all the comforts of home." He reached under the seat and brought up Trout's machine gun.

Pike started the engine.

Trout leaned over and turned it off.

"Did you see that?" Pike asked his friend.

Suggs said he had never seen anything like it in his life. "Show him."

Pike unzipped his ratty windbreaker and held its left side open. "This is dynamite," he said of what was sticking out of an inside pocket.

"We were on our way to blow our way into a video-game arcade," Suggs said. "Don't make us have to blow you up instead."

Pike zipped his windbreaker shut.

"We need to talk," Trout said. "For one minute."

"About what?" Pike asked.

"About what's in the back of the truck."

"I *know* what's in the back," Suggs said. "Color televisions."

Pike told Trout that the second Suggs spotted the truck he smelled color televisions.

"You're wrong," Trout said, wondering what he was going to say next. He couldn't tell them what was really back there. If he did, they would get ball bats and begin breaking out store windows and eventually reinforcements from another precinct would be dispatched to restore order.

These people had no self-discipline.

"Antiques?" Pike asked.

"No."

"New clothes? Designer jeans?"

"There's nothing in the back."

"That does it," Suggs said, wrestling with the machine gun. He got it stuck under the dashboard. Trout was concerned that Suggs would accidentally shoot somebody in the foot.

Trout told them that all they had to do was look in the back, if they didn't believe him.

"This is some kind of trick," Suggs said.

Pike told him to be quiet so he could think. He moved the wheel back and forth a few more times.

Trout glanced at the side-view mirror and wondered why Lovely wasn't doing anything helpful.

"This thing is full of big-screen Magnavoxes," Suggs said. "I'd stake my life on it."

Pike told Trout that he could talk some more.

Trout took a deep breath and told them that he had just stolen this truck from a warehouse not ten minutes from here. He said he had recently been released from prison and had been promised seventy-five hundred dollars for the delivery of the back-van part. He was going to keep the cab and paint it and use it to make an honest living. When they jumped him, Trout said, he was waiting for word on the police radio that an accident had been cleared from the highway he needed to use. He assured them that there was nothing in the van. All they had to do was look.

Trout's plan was to get everybody outside, where Lovely

could observe what was going on, and run over these two sons of bitches. Or if Lovely didn't want to do that, Trout could at least run.

"He's lying," Suggs said. "This is full of color televisions. *Consoles.*"

Trout took the keys out of the ignition and showed Pike which one unlocked the back doors.

"Okay, *there*," Suggs said.

"There what?" Pike wondered.

"If there's nothing in the back of this thing, then why would he lock it?"

"That's a good question," Pike said.

Trout started to agree. Instead he said that he had locked the back doors so nobody would steal them.

"That's a pretty good answer," Pike said.

Suggs said it was garbage.

"Damn!" Officer Buck said, falling.

When Pike opened the back doors of the van and stuck his head inside, Buck leaned down and chopped at the pistol with his left hand. Buck was in a tiny hammock made out of shirts and belts. As he hacked at the gun, he lost his balance and fell out of the sling he had stretched from hinge to hinge inside the van, just over the doors.

He fell directly on top of Pike.

Buck weighed 185 pounds.

Pike never knew what hit him.

Buck never knew what he hit.

Both lay dazed by the back doors.

Pike's top half was inside the van; his legs dangled outside.

The rest of the officers were huddled at the other end of the truck when Buck fell on Pike.

"Get him!" Lieutenant Bush shouted when he saw that one of their captors had been stunned.

Lieutenant Bush and three or four officers rushed toward the two fallen men.

"Good God," Suggs said when he saw something crash on his partner. At first Suggs didn't know what had fallen. He took Trout's machine gun from inside his coat and charged. He charged until he saw the police. He saw four uniformed officers, one man in his undershorts, and behind them, a woman.

Suggs had never seen anything like it.

He had never *dreamed* anything like it.

On the other hand, the police had never seen anything like Suggs either. Although he didn't feel too menacing, he looked it. Lieutenant Bush saw Suggs standing there with a machine gun and promptly fell to his stomach, as did the others behind him.

"*Liar*," Suggs screamed at Trout, who was hiding behind a light post.

Suggs dropped the machine gun and turned and ran, figuring they wouldn't shoot an unarmed man in the back.

Lieutenant Bush and Mounds and Sergeant House crawled forward and dragged the two unconscious men into the truck.

Suggs lost a shoe but kept running. He stumbled but kept running. His plan was to run until he came to water, and then jump.

Trout ran from behind the light post, fully expecting to be cut down. The police officers were expecting the same thing as they cowered together at the front of the truck, using the unconscious body of one of their previous captors as a shield.

Trout slammed the back doors on the truck, made a fist, and looked around for something to punch.

Suggs ran right by Lovely.

As he approached, Lovely rolled his window down and leaned outside and asked, "How's it going up there?"

Suggs's face was purple.

When he saw a truck identical to the one that had the police inside it, he screamed and veered to his right. He tripped over the far curb, crashed into a garbage can, and lay motionless on the sidewalk.

"Not that I care in the least," Lovely said to the body, rolling his window back up.

Nobody in the back of the truck knew exactly what to make of the situation, particularly Pike, who thought he had died and gone to hell, and was heartbroken to find out he hadn't.

"*Now* who's so smart," one of the officers said, shaking a stick of dynamite in Pike's face.

"Don't hit him with that," somebody said.

They had removed from Pike's person three sticks of dynamite, a hand grenade, two knives, a pistol, and a Dunhill cigarette lighter, which they used to see by.

"Nice going," somebody said to Officer Buck, who had a large knot on his forehead.

"Thanks. What'd I do?"

After everybody calmed down, Lieutenant Bush and Pike said almost simultaneously:

"*What's going on here?*"

"You bastards will never get away with this," Officer Buck said, rubbing his forehead.

Pike took a quick look around and tended to agree with those who had him. What *he* wanted to know was what the police department was doing in the back of a truck that was supposed to be full of color televisions. He also kind of wondered why he wasn't being transported to jail. And then there was the question of the man in his underwear.

The first thing Lieutenant Bush wanted to know was what Pike and his people had in mind.

"You mean me and Suggs?"

Lieutenant Bush had somebody write that down with a silver pen Pike had hidden in his sock.

"Me and Suggs was hoping to buy some color televisions."

"Suggs and I," Lieutenant Bush said.

"Suggs and you what?"

"Suggs and *I were* looking for some color televisions."

"I'll be damned," Pike said. "That Suggs, he gets around."

As it became apparent that neither man had the slightest idea what the other was talking about, Lieutenant Bush had Pike start from the beginning and explain, using reasonable English, his actions that morning.

"Me and Suggs," Pike said.

"Suggs and I," Lieutenant Bush said.

"Suggs and I, Suggs and I, Suggs and I!"

Lieutenant Bush nodded for Pike to continue.

"Him and me was walking down the street minding our own business when somebody fell on my head."

Officer Buck said either Pike could tell the truth or he had the right to remain silent. Forever.

"Okay, okay," Pike said, "but this won't stand up in no court of law."

Pike admitted that he and Suggs had been thinking about borrowing the van in which they sat. They thought the van might be full of something entertaining. The guy they had tried to *borrow* the truck from said it was empty. This guy said he had just stolen the truck and was taking it to another state. When Pike opened the back doors for a look, somebody fell on his head, and here he was, getting ready to file some kind of suit.

"You're not part of their organization?" Lieutenant Bush asked.

"Yeah," Pike said. "I'm their public relations man. What organization?"

The only other thing of interest Pike could tell the police was the location where they were parked.

Mounds bought Pike's story. "He's too messy to be one of them."

"Why would they keep us in the middle of town?" Sergeant House asked.

"What do you mean *keep?*" Pike said.

The van fell silent.

Pike said that what it looked like to him was that the police had been stolen; and this had *National Enquirer* written all over it. Pike said that for a few thousand dollars he'd never breathe a word to anybody.

Officer Buck regained some of his strength and put himself in charge of their newly acquired arsenal. He thought they should blow a hole in the side of the truck.

"It's no wonder the criminals are having a field day," Pike said. "*We'd* get blown to bits too."

Lieutenant Bush told everybody to hold it down. Since they had the company of a criminal, they might as well get some use out of it. He asked Pike if he had a reasonable suggestion about resolving their predicament.

"I got no idea," he said. "I usually break *into* things. That is, I did once, a long time ago. For which I was acquitted."

Lieutenant Bush told everybody that this much was clear: They were in a much better position now that Pike had arrived. They had some firepower. Although they still couldn't walk to the doors and knock them open, for fear of initiating a bloody exchange the likes of which this city hadn't seen in hours or maybe even days, they were still in a position of considerable strength should somebody attempt to open the doors from the outside.

With the dynamite and the pistol and the knives and the hand grenade, they were at least *competitive.*

As far as the doors were concerned, the people on both sides seemed to be at a standoff.

The morning shift would begin drifting into work at

around six A.M., so it was reasonable to conclude that their captors planned to try something fairly soon.

"What we could do," Lieutenant Bush said, "now that we have some bargaining power, is attempt to attract attention."

"Attract who?" Billows asked.

"A pedestrian, a janitor in a building."

"That's not half bad."

Lieutenant Bush told Billows that he needn't act so surprised.

Buck took Pike's pistol and began pounding the wall with the butt. A few people screamed for help.

"Hey," Heather said from the back doors. "Somebody out there is saying something."

"Quiet," Lieutenant Bush said.

"Shut up in there," Trout yelled.

"No," Lieutenant Bush shouted back.

"If you don't, I'll drive this damn truck into the river."

"Hold it down," Lieutenant Bush said.

Trout had to scream to be heard. He told everybody to get away from the doors. They did that, reluctantly.

"All things considered," Heather said, "I'd rather be where they are."

Three

The pay phone next to Trout finally rang.

He got out of the van and almost ripped the receiver from its socket, answering.

"Finch is ready to go," Annabel said.

"Well, what do you know," Trout said. "I was beginning to think I was going to get a sunburn doing this."

"Good luck."

"How's it going there?"

"You don't want to know. It's too depressing."

"You're right."

"See you in a little while," Annabel said.

Trout hung up and walked back to his truck.

His mood had improved all the way up to rotten since he had been jumped by the two sneak thieves. That the people in the van were armed wasn't the end of the world. Nor was it Good Friday. It was just there. All it really meant was that he couldn't check on them as originally planned. They were still locked in, though. What bothered Trout was that he hadn't thought to secure his doors while waiting for the all clear. Maybe screwing up was a trend. Maybe he had overlooked something else that would result in their being sent to prison.

But by whom?

Trout was pleased to receive the all clear. The guard had changed at the museum ten minutes before. All they had to do now was control a few more people and they would be home free.

He couldn't *wait* to get on private property.

They were too vulnerable on the streets.

Trout pulled his truck from the curb and moved carefully ahead to the intersection just in front of the museum's main gates. The museum was on up a pretty hill. He waited through several green lights. During this time one car went by, left to right. Otherwise the street that ran in front of the museum was deserted.

The mist was still nice and thick.

Trout checked his side-view mirror and saw that Lovely had moved forward with him. Nothing was hanging from Lovely's front bumper.

Trout sat through a third green light and pulled his gloves on. When the next red went off, he lurched forward, rolled through the three-pronged intersection, and approached the wrought-iron gate, which was about seventy-five yards on up the hill.

They could have gained access to the museum grounds in any number of ways, the majority of which would have been very dramatic. They could have dressed in black, and they could have swung over the fence on ropes tied to trees. They could have pole-vaulted in, or sailed in on hang gliders, or burrowed in. Not that it mattered. The grounds were like a mine field. There were wires scattered every few yards beneath the beautifully manicured turf. These wires were connected to people who were paid handsomely to guard a building that couldn't be broken into in the first place.

Trout thought a lot about how to get through the gates, before finally deciding to drive in.

What if somebody in a nearby building was standing at a window with binoculars? All they could do was call Annabel.

A big city made music, even in the short hours before dawn. Screeching tires were the strings. Crashing gates were from the percussion section.

So Trout drove to the gates, put the nose of his truck against the lock, and pushed. The wrought-iron gates were as much for show as for protection—there was even a camera hooked to the top—and they flew right open.

The gates then banged back against the front bumpers and fenders of the truck.

Trout looked back at the intersection where Lovely waited. It was otherwise clear, so he moved his truck onto museum property and stopped a few yards down the drive.

He got out to wait for Lovely and was invigorated by the cool morning mist.

I'll be damned, Lovely thought. No, I am *being* damned.

He wiped perspiration off his forehead and looked across the intersection at Trout, who was waving his right arm like a windmill.

Let's see here, Lovely thought, tilting the last drop of cherry vodka from the pint bottle. He spilled some on his shirt. He could turn left and speed directly for a friend's place up in Ontario. Trout would come after him, though, would track him down, even if it meant traveling to the most barren corners of the planet, and kill him. So Lovely forgot Ontario, it was too complicated. A check, that was the key. No cash. If Trout paid Lovely in cash, whoever killed him up at the museum would go through his pockets and get the thirteen hundred. A check would go to Lovely's estate, wouldn't it? That was better, more humane.

Lovely threw the empty pint bottle out his window—it crashed on the sidewalk—and proceeded through the iron gates exactly the way Trout had. The gates had settled back together. Lovely bumped them open, waited until they banged back against his front bumpers, and pulled up even with Trout's truck.

Trout trotted back to the gates and pushed them together so they would appear locked. He put a rock by the gates to hold them closed.

Now that they were safely on the property, it didn't matter if somebody from the other side of the fence saw the trucks. Things were frequently moved into and out of apartments and offices and museums in the middle of the night so those doing the moving could escape the chaos that soaked up the sunshine.

"I want my money," Lovely said. "I want a personal check for *fifteen* hundred."

They stood in the headlights from one of the trucks.

Trout made a face. "What's that smell?"

"What smell?" Lovely looked around, innocently.

"Waffle syrup. I smell blueberry waffle syrup."

"Oh, that. It's me I guess. I had an eye-opener."

Trout told Lovely he wasn't finished yet. "I can't drive *two* trucks up that hill."

"Is that the end of it?" Lovely asked, glancing at the museum.

Trout said it was.

The museum was flooded by lights at ground-level shining up into the fog. The entire top of the hill glowed.

Trout thought it was pretty.

Lovely said it reminded him of that Sherlock Holmes movie where the big dog ripped everybody's throat out.

94

"Follow me," Trout said.

"I'll follow you to hell," Lovely said about the top of the hill, "and not a step further."

Quackenbush watched the business at the front gates for almost a minute without realizing it was fact, not fiction.

He was the head of nighttime security at the museum.

He sat in an area that looked a little like the control room of a television station. The wall he faced was covered with miniature television screens, several dozen of them, showing live pictures of every inch of the grounds and every corner of the museum's twenty galleries. There was even a camera in the men's room so Quackenbush would be the first to know if somebody tried to tunnel in through the plumbing. Had somebody tried that, Quackenbush would actually have been the second to know. The police would have been the first. There were heat sensors underneath the museum. These sensors were connected to the master alarm, which had a direct tie-in to the authorities.

The security had been installed by people from Japan.

Cameras were everywhere.

Out front there were even cameras that did nothing but monitor other cameras.

Sometimes Quackenbush felt like a baked potato sitting in a microwave oven.

After the security system was installed, the man from Tokyo said that if anybody broke into this museum and got away with anything more than unpleasant memories, he would return to the grounds and cut off his right arm.

Quackenbush even got to attend a two-week seminar in Tokyo that concerned itself with the new security system and the modern thief and his or her habits. Quackenbush learned what you were supposed to be on the lookout for, when it came to running sophisticated gear like this.

You watched for people who might attempt to fly in

through the window and suspend themselves in midair with some variety of mini helicopter. You watched for people who might hide a small robot in the tank part of a toilet, then attempt to have the robot remove works of art by remote control after business hours.

But at no time during the seminar in Japan did any of the experts alert Quackenbush to the possibility that somebody might drive a big truck through the front gates.

So when it happened, it didn't quite register.

Quackenbush was a little sleepy and overconfident.

During the first few seconds of the mess at the gates, Quackenbush thought he was watching regular television. He had a small Sony black-and-white off to the right of his desk, and he thought he was watching a late movie instead of a shot from a front-gate camera inside a tree a third of the way up the hill.

The man in the first truck was not a bad actor.

The man in the second truck was a ham.

It wasn't until lights began flashing on his master panel that Quackenbush realized that this was no dumb movie.

He bolted upright in his chair and called for some close-ups on three or four of his outdoor cameras. He watched in disbelief as the two trucks stopped *inside the fence!* They weren't making any deliveries. And this wasn't the way you made deliveries. People with something to deliver rang the bell.

The alarms that were triggered the second the first truck bumped the gates were for the most part silent. Two alarms buzzed. Another hissed. The other five or ten flashed. Consequently, Quackenbush had to wake up his assistant, who was sleeping on a cot in the corner of the security room.

He woke his assistant by raking a coffee cup onto the floor.

Quackenbush's assistant was named Mickey. Mickey rolled off his cot and half stumbled to where Quackenbush sat staring at close-ups of the two men from the trucks.

"What's that?" Mickey asked.

"I don't know," Quackenbush said.

Mickey was a decent assistant. He had worked for Quackenbush for six months. He was big and strong and brave. He just didn't love art enough, yet. But he was coming around. Quackenbush gave Mickey a pop quiz once a week.

Quackenbush regarded the masterpieces he guarded as his children, and sometimes he spoke to them during his rounds.

Anybody trying to harm so much as the frame on a Chagall had bargained for much more than he imagined.

"It might be drunks," Quackenbush said as Mickey shielded his eyes from the red, blue, and green alarm lights flashing on the control board.

The only other thing Quackenbush could think of was that this might be some sort of test set up by the board of directors to see how security would react.

"They drive pretty straight for drunks," Mickey said as the first truck moved on up the hill. "No, I don't think they're drunks. They're criminals."

"All the alarms are registering," Quackenbush said calmly. "The police will be here in a matter of minutes."

"I know criminals when I see them," Mickey said. "I'm going to get some more guns so we can get them in a cross fire."

Quackenbush nodded.

In the fifteen years he had worked at the museum, the only thing that had been stolen was a paper-towel dispenser from one of the rest rooms. And that had been taken out of Quackenbush's check the next week.

If the men in the trucks planned on stealing so much as a shrub from around one of the statue-fountains out front, they had put their lives on the line.

"Stop where you are," Quackenbush said into a microphone.

His words came out of a speaker by a water sprinkler on the drive leading up to the museum.

Trout, who was in front, hit his brakes immediately and came to an even stop on the pavement.

Lovely veered right and ran into a dainty flower bed, sending petals flying.

Trout leaned out his window.

"You're being watched. Turn around this instant and move off the property. And be careful of those flowers."

Trout looked back at Lovely, who was resting his forehead on his steering wheel.

"What?" Trout asked.

"Leave the grounds. Don't move forward. Put your trucks in reverse and back out."

"What? I can't hear you," Trout said.

"They're criminals," Mickey said. "I checked those speakers the day before yesterday. They work perfect."

Mickey's voice came through the speaker.

Lovely sat up straight and began looking around for dogs.

"Are you a servant?" Trout asked.

Mickey said that nobody would ever mistake this for a private house.

"This is a museum," Quackenbush said. "I repeat, this is a museum. You're trespassing on private property. If you proceed, you do so at your own risk."

Trout shrugged, rolled his window up, and began moving his truck slowly forward again. He moved a few yards and waited for Lovely to catch up.

"They're coming to get us," Mickey said.

"We'll see," Quackenbush told him.

Annabel listened to the alarm from the museum for a few seconds. It was one of three dozen or so connected to places like banks where fortunes were kept overnight.

The alarm from the museum stayed on.

Annabel stubbed out her cigarette and typed into the computer the note that several squad cars had been dispatched to the museum, and that all was well.

Alarms in places with fortunes also showed up in the computers at police headquarters downtown.

Annabel typed in a message about how there had been a minor traffic accident by the front gates at the museum, but nobody had been injured.

Trout and Lovely parked their trucks near the front entrance.

Trout got out and walked to the door, which was gargantuan. It seemed to be made of redwood. Trout banged on the door a few times and put his ear to it.

"I want my money right this second," Lovely said. "I want a check for all but a hundred. I want some fives so I can get a cab."

"I don't have any fives," Trout said.

He beat on the doors again and shouted, "Come on, in there, open up."

"But you do have something for me. You have the envelope."

Trout nodded.

Lovely guessed he could always walk home. It was only nine miles.

"We're not done yet," Trout said, looking at his hands, which were sore.

Lovely said there must be some mistake. *He* was done. He had agreed to drive the truck to the top of the hill and he had done that, and now he was going to collect his *fifteen* hundred and buy himself a one-way ticket to somewhere much calmer, like Central America.

"You need to drive the trucks around to the other side of the building, Lovely. There's a small gravel parking lot over there. We need to get the trucks out of sight from the street. And we need to do it fast. You do that, and you can go home."

"Are you trying to break in there?"

Lovely looked at the museum. All the windows had thick bars over them.

"With your *fists?*"

"Attention," somebody from inside the museum said on another loudspeaker. This announcement came from beside the front door. "Attention, men from the trucks. You are in serious trouble. Forget the flowers you destroyed and leave the property at once. You have sixty seconds. The police are on their way and will be arriving momentarily."

Lovely looked up at the small speaker that was built into the bricks. "Listen to me very carefully," he said. "I don't know anything about this. This guy kidnapped my wife and kids and said he'd kill them unless I did what he said."

"Stand with your hands over your head," somebody from inside said.

"Right," Lovely said. "Don't shoot me."

He put his hands on his head.

Trout got a fair-sized rock from one of the flower beds and smashed the speaker to smithereens.

"You can put your hands down now," he said to Lovely. "And you can drive both trucks around to the far side of the building. Then you can go home."

✿ ✿ ✿

Lovely parked the first truck—the one Trout had driven —in the gravel parking lot. He pulled it next to a curb, made certain that there was no evidence in the cab, and trotted as fast as his stomach permitted to the other truck.

Trout was at a window, peeking inside the museum.

The sight of that only made Lovely's stomach burn more; so he quickly hopped into the remaining truck and drove it to a position beside the first vehicle.

Lovely climbed out of the cab and was startled by Trout, who was leaning against the building.

"Say," Trout said. The machine gun rested casually at his side, like a croquet mallet. "You messed it up. You pulled them in forward. We need them backed in so we can get out of here fast."

"We?"

"So back them out from the curb and rearrange them with the fronts pointing toward the front gates, okay?"

"I need two hundred more or I don't move."

"Okay. But hurry."

Lovely climbed back into one of the trucks but put the wrong set of keys in the ignition. "We're at a total of seventeen hundred."

Trout nodded and walked around front, where somebody from inside the museum was telling them, through another speaker back by a statue-fountain of a naked woman, to discard their weapons and stretch out flat on their stomachs.

Lovely wasn't too neat with his parking this time.

He went over a couple of curbs and mowed down a sapling while rearranging the first truck. To get it pointed the way Trout requested, he had to make a loop out front. He kicked up some gravel where Trout was standing with the machine gun.

It only took Lovely a few minutes to get the vans turned around. He didn't back them in. He made sweeps over the turf and entered the tiny parking lot from the rear, leaving in his wake some huge ruts and mangled bushes and shrubs.

Lovely returned to the front of the museum, gasping from stress and almost doubled over in pain—his stomach hurt—and he found Trout sitting calmly on the steps.

"I want two hundred more."

"Make it five," Trout said.

Lovely had the feeling he wasn't going to get paid for this.

Finch stopped at the front gates and felt sick. He got out and squinted up the hill at the museum, wondering where the two trucks were.

Had Trout been captured?

Already?

Finch walked to a cement pillar that was to the left of the gates. He opened a black box and lifted a telephone off a rack. When someone answered at the other end, Finch said, "Hello, hello, this is the police."

Quackenbush wished he had brought his sunglasses to work with him. The alarm boards were blinding. The alarm out front had just gone off, which indicated that somebody had been tampering with the door. That light was orange. Quackenbush winced as four more lights began flashing. These alarms were hooked to the paintings in the front hallway. Mickey had been sent there to remove the Picassos, in case there was gunplay inside the museum.

Quackenbush finally agreed with his assistant; somebody, be it a drug addict or whoever, most definitely wanted to get into the museum.

And Quackenbush was *appalled*.

"The gates are open," he said into his end of the telephone. "The gates are open because two people just drove trucks through them."

Quackenbush watched the police officer on one of the television screens.

"Huh?" Finch said, holding a hand over his free ear.

Mickey stuck his head into the control room and reported that he had set up a barricade at the end of the front hallway using an eighteenth-century love seat as a shield.

"Idiot," Quackenbush said.

"Huh?" Finch said again.

"Use the leather sofa from the Rembrandt Room."

"But hell, bullets will go right through the leather," Mickey said.

"The gates are open," Quackenbush repeated to Finch.

Finch made a face. He held the phone away from his ear, shook his head, and said for what Quackenbush guessed to be the tenth time that he was the police.

"I can see that," Quackenbush said simply and almost hopelessly. For an instant he felt more hostility toward the police than he did toward the man who was trying to beat in the front door.

"Hello, up there, I can't hear much," Finch said. "This is the police. What's all that buzzing. What's all that screeching? What's the problem up there?"

"Alarms," Quackenbush said.

"Huh?"

"Alarms, damn it. *Burglar* alarms. We're under direct frontal attack."

Finch smiled and asked the security man to please repeat that.

The quick grin was another of the things Quackenbush was having a hard time believing.

"Where are their vehicles?"

"Around to the side."

"What?"

"By the side of the damn building."

"How many perpetrators are there?"

"Why don't you come up and see for yourself?"

"Please repeat."

"If you'd get your butt up here, there wouldn't *be* any perpetrators. You could stop them before they perpetrated. The gates are open."

"Hang on," Finch said.

He strolled to the gates and shoved them open.

More alarm lights went on as Mickey removed priceless works of art from the walls adjacent to the front doors.

Quackenbush thought about clubbing the alarm lights out.

He thought about clubbing his own lights out.

"These gates are open," Finch said.

"I know." Quackenbush sighed.

He watched the police officer move onto the property.

Mickey yelled from the hallway that the paintings were safely stored in a closet. Quackenbush knew that. The closet alarm light, which was purple, had just begun flashing on the master board.

All the colors together were pretty in their own perverse way.

Quackenbush's plan was to continue monitoring the situation in the security room and then join Mickey at the barricade if the outer line of defense, the front door, was penetrated.

He watched the police officer, whose total in-the-field experience must have been acquired during the drive over, stop his squad car just inside the front gates to check the tires for air.

He watched the two lunatics from the trucks confer by the fountain out front.

He told Mickey not to open fire until he gave the word.

"What word?" Mickey asked nervously from behind the leather sofa he had tilted over in the hall.

"Fire," Quackenbush said.

"Okay," Mickey said.

Quackenbush removed his revolver from his holster and put it on the table in front of the television screens.

He was not going to be taken alive by either the perpetrators or the board of directors.

Trout sat down beside Lovely on a cement bench by the statue-fountain of a naked woman and told his neighbor that things were not quite as dangerous as they seemed.

"Is that a siren?" Lovely asked. He was bent over forward.

"Yeah," Trout admitted. "But it's one of ours."

Lovely said his stomach was killing him.

"It's that crap you drank."

"That, the siren, the trucks—all of it."

Trout bent forward so he could converse on Lovely's level without having to shout. He said he wished Lovely could have gone home before he found himself in the middle of all this.

"I need an ambulance," Lovely said softly.

"That's out of the question," Trout told him.

"Then shoot me."

Trout removed an envelope from his back pocket and shook it so Lovely could hear the bills sliding around inside. "The original thousand is in there. It's all I have on me. You can take it and go, and I'll get the rest to you later. Or you can hang around until after the fake shoot-out and take the rest of what you've got coming in merchandise."

"Fake *shoot-out*," Lovely said flatly.

"Yeah," Trout said, patting Lovely's tired back. "It's nothing to worry about. We're using blanks."

"*Merchandise?*"

"From the museum. A painting or something like that. A Matisse. They're real nice. You've got what, twelve more hundred coming? The doorknobs inside are worth that."

The siren from the police car tearing up from the front gates was getting louder. Its red lights were starting to bounce off the museum.

"I can't run," Lovely said. "I can't even roll."

Trout helped Lovely to his feet and led him by the elbow to a group of shrubs that had not been flattened by the trucks. Trout piled some leaves toegther in the middle of the bushes and made Lovely a nice little nest.

"It'll all be over in a few minutes."

"I'll never forget you for this," Lovely said, lowering himself onto the bed of leaves.

"It's okay."

"It wasn't a compliment."

Quackenbush took back everything he had said or thought about the police officer. The man made one of the greatest shots Quackenbush had ever seen anywhere, including old western movies where four outlaws were sometimes brought under control with one bullet.

Finch got going too fast coming up the drive and almost skidded into the right front corner of the museum. He had not practiced this part in the fog and had a hard time judging distances. He hit the brakes and fishtailed and kicked up a large cloud of dust and gravel.

He jumped out of the squad car and shouted, "Where is everybody?"

Trout ran out of the dust carrying a revolver that was full of blanks. The half dozen times they had practiced this part, there was no damn dust, either. Trout fired the revolver at the cloud, mostly to let Finch know where he was.

Finch stumbled out of the dust onto the front steps of the museum, coughing.

"He's been hit," Mickey said, watching a monitor.

"There's no blood," Quackenbush said.

Finch took his hat off and waved away some of the dust.

He located Trout, who was hiding behind the statue-fountain of the naked woman.

"Stop where you are," Finch shouted, drawing the revolver full of blanks from its holster.

I'm already stopped, for God's sake, Trout thought. He stood and fired another blank at Finch. Then he turned and ran. He ran for a clump of trees about a hundred yards away.

"Stop," Finch said again.

Trout continued running, as planned.

Finch aimed his pistol at Trout and attempted to pull the trigger, but nothing happened. He looked at the gun and shook it. He moved the safety catch left and right and tried the trigger again as Trout moved nearer the trees. The trigger wouldn't budge.

Trout, who should have been shot at by now, began slowing down. By the time he ducked in behind the first tree trunk, he was almost walking.

Finch tossed the worthless gun into a flower bed and removed from inside his shirt a pistol containing real bullets. He was aware that he was being watched from inside the museum, and he couldn't think of anything better to do than fire a live round in the general direction of the tree behind which Trout crouched.

Finch made a point of firing high.

"Heads up," he yelled first.

Trout was peeking around the trunk when Finch sent a real bullet spiraling toward him. The bang from the gun and the loud *crack!* over Trout's head occurred almost simultaneously.

That's . . . Trout thought; but he never had a chance to think *better.*

The bullet tore into the tree a few inches above Trout's head.

Bark flew.

Trout fell.

Oh, Christ, Finch thought: I've killed him.

The guards were lured out of the museum, though, as planned.

Quackenbush swung the heavy front door open and found Finch standing limply with the pistol at his side.

"Don't forget that other one in the bushes," Mickey said. "The fat one."

"Come out with your hands up," Quackenbush shouted at the shrubs. "Come out and step *around* the shrubs."

"Okay, okay, don't kill me." Lovely struggled to his feet and wobbled out of the bushes with leaves hanging all over him. He shuffled toward the front door and leaned against the frame so Quackenbush could frisk him.

"Hold this," Quackenbush said, handing Finch a rifle.

"What *is* all this?" Lovely asked anybody.

"I've shot him," Finch said. "I murdered him."

Lovely said that was the best news he had heard all night. "I'm on *your* side," he told Quackenbush, who said it would all come out at the trial.

The four of them walked down the hill to check out the body and see what they needed to call—an ambulance or a hearse.

"You have to look at it this way," Quackenbush said, placing his hand on Finch's shoulder. "There's no telling how many lives you saved by removing that madman from society. You should feel proud, if anything."

After they had walked halfway to where Trout lay in a heap, Finch's mood improved appreciably. Although he had pumped a live round at his friend, there was no hard evidence to suggest that Trout was actually *dead*. Finch stopped them a few yards from the body and told everybody to stay back. He approached Trout, who was facing the other way. He grabbed Trout's shoulder and rolled him over.

"A head shot," Mickey said. "Unbelievable."

Trout's forehead had some blood on it.

Finch sat down and put an ear to Trout's chest. The heartbeat was faint, but it wasn't playing chopsticks. It was fairly regular. "He's *alive*," Finch said.

"It's probably better that way," Quackenbush said with a shrug. "This way, he can give testimony about what happens to people who try to break into museums."

Finch said they were, by God, back in business. He picked up a weapon with each hand like a gunslinger and pointed them at Quackenbush and his partner. "Don't move."

"He's no cop," Lovely said. "He's one of *them*."

"Sit down," Finch said.

Mickey sat down.

Quackenbush thought about it. Mickey reached up and pulled at his boss's sleeve. "If they'd shoot *each other* to make this look good, God only knows what they'd do to us."

Quackenbush sat down.

Finch held Trout's left wrist and felt a steady enough pulse.

Lovely studied the situation and walked around to stand beside Finch.

"I was only kidding before, I'm with these guys," he said.

Finch considered his options and discarded them one by one like remnants of a busted inside straight.

He couldn't leave Trout.

He couldn't leave the guards.

He couldn't just sit there.

The sun would come up eventually.

So he dispatched Lovely on a very important mission: Lovely was to haul himself up the hill to the squad car and call in the message that meant the museum was theirs. Finch told Lovely exactly what to say. He called to Lovely's attention the fact that the squad car was positioned in such a way that Lovely's fat rump would be in sight at all times.

"And you already know what kind of shot I am," Finch said.

He told Lovely to walk up the hill, reach inside the police car, remove the microphone from the dash, push the button, and state his little speech clearly and without hysteria. "Come back and you get this," said Finch, waving the envelope with the thousand dollars at Lovely again.

"I've heard *that* before," Lovely said. "And that's only part of it. Me and Audie Murphy here put together some new numbers."

Lovely looked down at Trout, who was in no shape to verify the negotiations.

"We're up to in the neighborhood of twenty-five hundred."

Finch nodded.

"Isn't that right, sport?" Lovely said down to Trout. "I got more than another thousand coming."

Trout said nothing.

"If he said it, it's good," Finch told Lovely. "He's going to be fine. We'll go over it when he comes around."

"Comes around," Lovely repeated. "I've seen better-looking sides of beef."

Finch motioned to Lovely, who approached reluctantly. Finch whispered into his ear, "I know what you're thinking. You're thinking you can get on the police radio and call in some kind of message for help without me knowing it, come back here, and get your money and then beat it."

"I'm thinking that now," Lovely said.

"Be quiet. *We're* on the other other end of that police radio. You understand what I'm saying?"

"You're everywhere."

"Let's go."

Finch walked Lovely about a third of the way toward the squad car. The guards remained seated on the ground near Trout.

"I have a plan," Mickey said.

"Be quiet down there," Finch half shouted.

"What is it?" Quackenbush asked. "But I don't like it already."

"We buy in with them."

That was not as sorry a plan as Quackenbush had expected.

"Hello," Lovely said into the microphone in the police car. The lights on top were still flashing.

Annabel frowned at the console through which calls from squad cars arrived. She looked at her watch. It was time for the all clear from the museum. The call was, in fact, a little late. But it wasn't supposed to begin like a call from your uncle.

After Lovely said "Hello," he scowled and said "No scratch that."

He let go of the button on the microphone and sent his mind back through time to when Finch had explained the terminology he was supposed to begin the call with. That this explanation had been given only a couple of minutes ago was inconceivable. Time no longer had any relevancy. The whole evening had exploded and the most burning memories were out of sequence. Mercenaries, Lovely guessed, guys who fought tooth and nail with knives, did a lot less work for hundreds of thousands of dollars.

"This is David Three," Lovely said proudly.

"Go ahead," Annabel said, wondering how Finch had lost his squad car. But she didn't panic because the person who had Finch's vehicle knew the David Three identification number. She doubted anybody would have tortured the car's identification number out of Finch. Therefore she reasoned that Finch had given the number to somebody of his own volition and for a very good reason. So Annabel, who was known for displaying almost inhuman resolve in times of great stress, sat quietly and waited for the all-clear signal or an explanation of why a goddamn stranger was in Finch's police car.

"This is David Three," Lovely said again. "Can you hear me or what?"

"Take your hand off the microphone," Annabel said. "Take your thumb off the button."

With his thumb on the button, Lovely couldn't hear her.

All he could hear was the blood rushing through his head.

"Can anybody out there hear me? Oh, God, what's going on? Somebody is supposed to answer."

Lovely looked at the keys in the ignition and considered making a run for it. He looked at Finch who was down the hill, pointing a rifle in his direction. If Lovely started the car and made a run for the gate, the tires would be shot out. The car would probably roll and explode. Not bad, Lovely thought of this option.

"Listen, damn it," he said into the microphone, his thumb still on the button. "This isn't funny. I'm only doing what I was told. Will somebody please answer me?"

"I can't while your thumb is on the button," Annabel said.

"Well, anyway, it's all clear here at the museum."

Lovely jammed the microphone back onto its holder on the dashboard.

Annabel took a puff off her forty-third cigarette of the last two hours and gave the person in Finch's squad car a second or two to get his hand away from the microphone. Then she said:

"We're having trouble receiving from your unit, David Three. The trouble seems to be in the red button on your microphone. You might hit it a couple of times and *let it go*. Please verify. Did we have an all clear from the museum?"

Lovely was outside the squad car. He leaned back in through the window and took the microphone from its rack.

"Yeah?" he said.

He depressed the button several times, and Annabel once.

"Confirm . . . museum . . . you," the voice from the radio said.

"What?" Lovely asked, letting go of the button.

"Please keep your stupid damn thumb off the button and confirm the report you just sent from the museum."

"Oh, yeah, right. This is David Three. It's all clear at the museum."

"Good," Annabel said.

"Say, listen." Lovely gave the okay sign to Finch, who was waving his rifle.

"Yes," Annabel said, imagining what this conversation sounded like to all the people sitting in their living rooms, listening to their police radios. That was a very popular hobby. People liked to listen to reports of accidents and crimes, then hop in their cars and go and look at some blood. Fortunately, there were dozens of museums in the city, and fortunately, it was around one thirty in the morning.

"This is David Three here again."

"Go ahead."

"Is somebody else coming here?"

"A backup will be on the way."

Lovely looked back to where Finch stood with the rifle, and where Trout lay bleeding from the head.

"Somebody might ought to bring along some Excedrin," Lovely said.

"Okay," Annabel said.

"Okay," Lovely said.

"Fine," Annabel said.

"Swell," Lovely said. "Bye."

Annabel and Roebuck closed the Thirty-third Precinct. They turned off all the lights and locked the doors and scrambled the computers some to make it seem as though they were malfunctioning temporarily.

Then they went out the back way and drove to the museum in a police car.

Roebuck did the driving.

He set his jaw and drove fast. He sailed through red lights and screeched around corners.

"Maybe they're in trouble," Roebuck said. "Maybe that's why somebody else called in." He pounded his fist on the steering wheel.

And he had been doing so well too.

They made half of the ten-minute drive in, Annabel guessed, forty-five seconds.

Finch and Lovely helped Trout up the hill.

Each person got an arm.

A third of the way up, Trout opened his eyes and moaned.

The way he felt reminded him of a cheap paperback he had read recently.

The book began:

It was the worst day of my life. I was dead.

For a while there, Trout didn't know where he was or what had happened to him.

He knew that something terrible had happened because he couldn't turn his head or hear much out of his left ear.

But by the time he got to the museum, he was able to swear lightly again.

Trout sat propped against a wall just inside the front door.

When he opened his eyes, Finch's face was about a foot away.

"The gun with blanks didn't work, so I had to shoot at you with the other gun," Finch said. "But it's okay. It worked. Your plan worked. We're in perfect shape."

Trout looked at the guards, who were seated across the hall from him.

"You got some bark on your temple there, but you look fine, Trout. Honest to God, the color's already coming back into your cheeks."

Trout touched his right cheek and showed Finch what was causing the color.

It was blood.

"So anyway," Finch said pleasantly, changing the subject, "I got all the alarms turned off in the security room. Lovely called the precinct and they're on their way. Everything is under control."

Trout touched his head.

"Damn near."

Finch said that what he was going to do now was turn off the lights on the squad car and then come back inside and start dragging masterpieces into the front hallway and get ready for the loading.

He turned and walked to the front door, which was open.

"Finch," Trout said. Then he said "Oh" and put his fingers to his eyes. His eyeballs hurt more than anything. "Stay away from the trucks."

Finch frowned.

"I mean, don't open the back of either one."

"You *do* know where you are."

Finch walked back toward Trout.

"While I was sitting around waiting for your all clear," Trout said slowly, "two men jumped me. They opened the truck. The police dragged one of them inside. The other one ran off."

Finch whistled.

"So now the police back there have some guns and things."

"*Things?*"

"Dynamite," Trout said.

"Who the hell jumped you, the National Guard?"

"Bums," Trout said.

"I'll be right back." Finch walked outside, closing the door behind him.

"My God," Mickey said.

Quackenbush grabbed his assistant's wrist and squeezed. Mickey nodded and whispered, "Where's the key?"

"My pocket," Quackenbush whispered back.

"Swallow it."

"It's on a big ring."

"What's all that whispering about?" Trout asked. He was still sitting near the front door. He was also still having a little trouble hearing and had to turn his head to hear Quackenbush's answer, which was:

"Nothing."

"What?" Trout pointed his right ear at the guards.

"Nothing."

"It was something. I heard it."

"We were talking about what a good idea this was," Mickey said. "We were talking about asking you if we could buy in."

"You can't," Trout said.

Mickey shrugged. "It's still a hell of an idea. You've got the police in the other truck out there, right?"

"What?"

"A great idea."

"Thanks," Trout said.

This conversation was interrupted by a knock on the front door. The first few knocks were light. Trout's bad ear was toward the door, so he didn't hear anything.

"Say," Quackenbush said loudly. "I think the guy outside wants something."

Trout turned his right ear to the door, nodded, and told the guards not to move.

"Follow my lead," Quackenbush said.

"I will until you get shot," Mickey said.

"Be quiet," Trout said.

116

"We are," Quackenbush said pleasantly.

"I saw your lips move."

Trout stood up, steadied himself, and moved to the front door. He took the knob and turned it. The knob moved, but the door didn't open. Trout let go of the knob and watched it move some more, as Finch was wrestling with it from the outside.

Presently, the door vibrated.

Finch pounded on it three times from the outside.

Trout pounded back three times.

Finch pounded twice.

Trout pounded twice.

"God damn it, let me in," Finch screamed.

Trout heard Finch the second time he screamed that. He could hear better by putting a finger in the ear that was still ringing.

"Let me out," Trout screamed.

"Let me in," Finch screamed.

They pounded on the door some more. After they quit pounding, Trout heard some noise behind him. He turned from the door and looked at the spot where the two guards had been sitting.

They were gone.

Their footsteps, running down a hallway, were loud at first; they stopped after a half a minute.

With Quackenbush in the lead, the guards ran through a gallery full of Manets and down some stairs to a basement hallway. They trotted to the back side of the museum and crept up some stairs that led to a storage room beside the kitchen that was at the end of the main hallway they had just left. There were brooms and things in this storage room, and plenty of file cabinets to hide behind.

Their plan was to remain quiet and club somebody when the opportunity presented itself.

Trout started to chase the guards but quickly came up

with a much better idea. After he had pointed his pistol at the eight or nine gallery doors opening off the main hallway, he raised the gun and put the barrel to his right temple.

Unless he thought of something fast, he was going to pull the trigger.

"Rip out the phone wires," Trout shouted with his mouth near the crack where the gigantic front door closed against its frame.

"What?" Finch said. "What? What?"

They each listened and then shouted at the crack where the door closed.

"The guards are loose. They ran away. You have to rip out all the wires so they can't call for help."

"How?" Finch asked.

"With your hands."

"I mean, how will I know which wire is which?"

"Rip them *all* the hell out."

"Okay, okay," Finch shouted.

"Have Lovely cover the back door."

Trout didn't hear a reply for a bit.

"He won't," Finch said, eventually.

"Then take your gun out and shoot him in the goddamn head. You ought to be pretty good at it by now."

After another pause, Finch said Lovely had consented to sit around back for three hundred dollars more.

"Kill him," Trout shouted.

Finch was away from the door a couple of seconds.

He returned and yelled, "He'll do it for a hundred."

"Pay him."

"Hey, Trout."

"What."

"It's all going to hell, isn't it. This whole thing is going to hell with us in the middle."

"No," Trout said.

"You didn't say that very confidently."

"All we've got to do is hang on, Finch." Trout was getting a sore throat from yelling on top of everything else. "It's still the same idea."

"We hang on?"

"Yeah," Trout yelled. "This small crap that goes wrong doesn't matter. It's a detour. It's the basic idea that's going to carry us through. You understand?"

"We can't worry about this small stuff."

"That's exactly right, Finch."

Finch was quiet a few seconds.

"Finch?"

"I'm here."

"Don't you *dare* go home."

"It's going to hell, but it doesn't matter. Is that basically where we're at right now?"

"Yeah," Trout yelled feebly.

"Right. I'm still in."

Finch found a lot of wires to pull.

The building was old and there were wires all over the place. There were wires running out of windows and into the ground, and wires leading into some kind of box by a toolshed out back, and wires stapled to the sides of the museum.

Finch didn't know what a telephone wire looked like, so he pulled whatever he could find, including a handful of wires that went underground to a post in the middle of the enormous back lawn.

He went at the wires for approximately five minutes.

Trout was sitting on a magnificently carved love seat in the main hallway, thinking, when the lights went out.

119

The lights didn't go dim.
They went off, all at once.
Poof.
Like that, as if somebody had blown them out.

Trout took an ashtray off a desk in the security room and smashed out a window. He wasn't concerned in the least about cutting a vein open. He took the ashtray and brought it back over his shoulder and hit the window as hard as he could. The window glass was thick, but it broke.

"*Finch,*" Trout yelled with his face against the bars that covered the outside of the window. He tried the bars and guessed that each one was anchored up in the rafters and down into the ground. The bars were strong.

Finch arrived out of breath and reported that Lovely was set up by the back door with a rake he had found in a toolshed.

"You know, it makes sense," Finch said, composing himself. "Somebody could hide in there and then club the guards after the place closed and lug off a lot of priceless stuff. So it makes sense to have the doors open with a key from either side."

"Be quiet and get the police car," Trout said. "Pull it up here and turn the brights on so I can see a little."

"That's a great idea. When Annabel and Roebuck get here, we can drive one of the cars through that damn front door."

Trout said no, they couldn't do that.

"Why?" Finch asked.

"There are steps out front."

"Oh, yeah, right," Finch said.

Trout reached through the bars and took Finch's flashlight and said that what he was going to do now was go look for the guards. "Why the hell did you rip the lights out?"

"These wires don't have name tags, Trout. I wasn't even yanking anything when they went out. Maybe the guards unplugged a fuse or something like that."

Finch went to pull the squad car around so Trout would have some light, at least in the security room and the hallway connecting to it.

Trout went to look for the guards, who were at least unarmed, unless you counted chairs or picture frames that weighed seventy-five pounds, or perhaps even swords from one of the galleries.

Trout made a left in the hallway and walked all the way to the end of it and checked things out there.

The last door on the left led to a kitchen.

Trout went in and peeked out a window by the back door. He waved his flashlight at Lovely, who ducked behind a tree.

The galleries opening off the main hallway were large rooms full of large paintings. There were no hiding places in any of these six or seven rooms, so Trout went through a gallery containing some gorgeous Gauguins to a staircase.

The stairs were in the middle of the building, Trout guessed.

He stood on the bottom step and shined his flashlight up to the landing above.

"Okay, it's over," he said. "We've got the doors covered. Come on out and nobody's going to get hurt."

Trout turned his right ear to the stairs and listened in case anybody surrendered.

Nobody did.

Trout checked a bathroom under the stairs and a closet off to the right, which was no fun, and then he went up to the second floor.

❋ ❋ ❋

Annabel held the wrought-iron gates open while Roebuck gunned the police car through.

She pushed the gates back together and propped them closed with the rock.

"I don't want to upset you," Roebuck said as Annabel slid back into the passenger seat up front. "But look."

Roebuck nodded up the hill.

"Where?" Annabel asked.

"That's my point. It's dark."

"Let's leave," Annabel said. "Let's go back to my place and watch the late movie."

Roebuck said they couldn't do that. *Could* they?

Annabel flicked a cigarette out her window.

"I wonder why it's so dark?" Roebuck asked.

"God only knows."

"Maybe we ought to ask Him. Hope for some kind of vision."

They sat there a few seconds staring at the night.

"Save your breath," Annabel said. "He's nowhere near here."

Roebuck put the car in gear and drove on up the hill. He was moving at a pretty good clip when a man leaped into his path from an evergreen to the right of the driveway. The man leaped into the headlights, waving his arms frantically.

"*Look out*," Annabel said, bracing herself against the dashboard.

Roebuck jerked the steering wheel sharply to the left and hit the brakes. He skidded around sideways and came to a stop.

"That's the worst driving I've ever seen," Annabel said, looking back at the person who had jumped from behind the bush.

"What are you talking about? I missed him."

"I know. It was Finch."

❈   ❈   ❈

Finch felt a little like a doctor with bad news as he gave it to them straight from the hip. He lowered his head and pawed at the ground with his right foot.

"You *what?*" Annabel said, pulling her arm away.

"Shot him," Finch said, lowering his head even more to show he hadn't *meant* to.

"*What?*"

"I shot him. Keep your voice down."

"You're kidding," Roebuck said.

"You *what?*"

"Shot him, shot him. In the damn head."

"How come?" Roebuck asked.

"The gun with blanks didn't work, so I had to shoot a live round at him. The bullet hit a tree and knocked some bark into Trout's head. It was an accident, but it happened, and that's all there is to it."

"How come you didn't shoot him in the leg or somewhere like that?" Roebuck asked.

"But he's up and around."

Annabel took a long puff on her cigarette, reducing its length by about half.

"There's one more thing," Finch said in the same tone he had used to explain how he had shot Trout near the head.

"There can't be," Annabel said.

"Two thieves jumped Trout earlier. One of them opened the back of the van and was dragged inside by the police. So they're armed."

"Who is?" Roebuck asked.

"The police. But they're still locked in the truck, so we're basically okay there."

Annabel asked if anything had been loaded yet. About a third of the artwork was supposed to have been loaded by the time Annabel and Roebuck left the precinct.

Finch quickly explained why nothing had been loaded.

"Trout's locked in and I'm locked out."

Roebuck stretched and looked up at the mist.

Annabel flicked an ash off her cigarette.

"They've got a trick door up there. The guards ran off, but Trout has gone after them."

"Where?" Annabel asked, pressing her fingers to her temples. Her cigarette dangled from her lips.

"Inside."

Annabel opened her left hand and counted off everything she needed to arrange neatly in her mind.

The police were armed.

"The police plus the one they dragged inside."

Trout had been shot in the head.

"More like grazed."

Everybody was locked in or out and the guards were loose.

"And nothing has been loaded. Don't yell at Trout, because he still doesn't feel so good."

Annabel flicked her cigarette into the grass and walked to their squad car.

"Don't you think you should get that," Finch said of the glowing cigarette butt. "It's evidence."

"Evidence? *What* evidence? There's been no crime committed here."

Four

The galleries upstairs were smaller.

Trout stood at the top of the stairs and shined his flashlight at the doors to a couple of these tiny galleries.

The flashlight was getting dim.

Trout banged it on some wooden railing at the top of the stairs.

The flashlight stayed dim.

He stood there and listened to Finch yell in through the window of the security room. Finch's voice echoed loudly. He reported that Annabel and Roebuck had arrived and that all was well outside. Nobody had come out. He wondered how it was going inside.

"Quit yelling at me," Trout yelled down the stairs. His ear had stopped ringing. "I don't want them to know where I am, okay?"

"I thought *you* were chasing *them*," Finch yelled.

Trout walked into a gallery full of pottery. This gallery

had doors on all four walls. Trout shined his light around and walked slowly to his left, pausing to look under a table.

"Let's go," he said without much feeling, just in case the guards were nearby.

He shook his flashlight. There seemed to be one lightning bug under the glass lens, one *old* lightning bug.

The light was yellow.

Trout walked from the gallery full of pottery into a gallery full of rugs hung on walls, where he made a right into a room full of oriental vases. There, his flashlight began flickering on and off.

Trout knelt down and banged the back of the flashlight on the wood floor.

The flashlight flickered twice more and went out.

"Damn," Trout said.

"*Trout*," Finch screamed.

Trout didn't answer.

He stood up and felt his way around a table to a door, and stopped. It didn't seem to be the door he had just entered. Trout found this all very unfair. His temple still throbbed slightly from when the tree bark had hit it and that, combined with the darkness, made him feel quite lost.

He called out for Finch.

Finch said, "Yeah."

The voice was to his left a little, so Trout moved that way in search of the stairs.

"Nothing," he told Finch.

Trout walked four steps and bumped into a wall. He felt his way along this wall to yet another damn door and stood in the middle of it. He shook the flashlight but nothing happened. He put it in his pocket and removed his pistol from his belt. He pointed the pistol toward the roof and fired it once. The noise was deafening. Plaster fell. In the flash from the end of the gun barrel, Trout was able to determine that he was back in the gallery with the pottery, which made the stairs left, didn't it? Whatever, he walked calmly toward that door.

When he was about halfway there, somebody behind Trout shouted:

"Drop it, you son of a bitch!"

Trout whirled and fired and fell. Pieces of pottery and wood flew all over the place. After Trout fired five times and fell, he rolled across the floor and banged into a table, knocking down four or five pots, one of which was heavy and landed on the middle of his back.

Trout managed not to scream and lay quietly on the floor.

"That ought to confuse them," Mickey whispered.

Quackenbush shrugged.

"Should I do it again?" Mickey stood beside a speaker on a wall of the storage room.

Quackenbush shook his head no.

Mickey wanted to go after the bastards.

"Our first obligation is to the art," Quackenbush whispered. "We have to stay put."

Mickey wanted to put a fuse back in and flick the lights on and off a few times. He wanted to scare the hell out of them.

Quackenbush had his assistant get back behind a file cabinet.

"Trout," Finch called out again.

"The more shots the better," Roebuck said. "If they jumped him at close range, one would have done it."

Annabel said nothing.

She stood by the broken window with her arms folded.

"Getting mad doesn't accomplish anything," Finch said.

"What does?" Annabel asked sourly.

Finch called for Trout again.

This time, there was an answer. It was weak. Trout's answer was:

"I'm alive."

"Did you get one of them?" Finch asked.

"No," Trout weakly.

"Did they shoot back?"

"No."

"Well then listen, Trout, you're in big trouble. You shot at them six times. You're out of bullets."

"Damn it to hell," Trout said, turning his flashlight off. It had come on with enough light for Trout to determine what he had just shot at. He had shot at the voice that came out of an intercom on the wall. He had missed the intercom. And now that everybody knew he was out of bullets, he couldn't turn the flashlight back on because somebody might throw a spear at it.

Trout had no choice except to feel his way through the small galleries to the middle of the museum and find the stairs. He was doing brilliantly until he backed into a mobile called *Man's Inner Struggles.* When that happened he was certain that one of the guards had him by the neck. *Man's Inner Struggles* was from France. It was heavy, particularly the base of the thing, which was a steel egg. Tiny blades extended upward from the egg. These blades were connected by thin wires to jagged pieces of stainless steel. The jagged pieces represented love and hate and fear and other emotions, and they dangled at about eye level.

Trout backed right into the middle of the mobile and took a couple of swings at it. One of the emotions wrapped itself around his right forearm, almost cutting off his circulation.

"They've got me," Trout shouted.

He continued to lash out with his free hand, his left, but

128

succeeded only in ripping the mobile off its base, which started rolling wildly around the room.

It seemed to Trout that the only chance he had was to keep moving, but as he did, more wires wrapped themselves around his shoulders, neck and ankles. The sculpture dragged along behind him, banging into table legs and door frames and what Trout guessed was a large urn, which shattered like a plate-glass window.

Somehow, Trout stayed upright.

He dropped his flashlight, which was no great loss, and blundered onto the stairs. He grabbed the handrail and began hopping down one step at a time.

The egg-shaped base caught up with Trout on the third stair from the top and passed him there, yanking his feet out from under him and dragging him the rest of the way down.

Trout fell over the egg on the ground floor, scrambled to his feet and ran for all he was worth toward a patch of light reflecting off a wall to his left.

He ran into the security room, screaming and flailing his arms at the wires and prongs that still had him.

Finch, Annabel, and Roebuck stood at the window in the glow of the headlights from the squad car, looking extremely concerned.

"Hold still," Annabel said.

Roebuck had found some pliers in the trunk of one of the police cars, and Annabel was reaching in through the bars, clipping wires.

The first wire she clipped was around Trout's neck.

It left a red mark.

Roebuck thought Trout looked like the Tin Man, but didn't say so.

"It's like a dungeon in there," Trout said calmly. "A *big* dungeon."

"Did you find the guards?" Finch asked.

"Yeah, they were taking a shower. They'll be along in a minute."

Annabel clipped a wire from around Trout's chest.

Nobody said anything during the remainder of the clipping.

After Annabel was finished, she leaned up and gave Trout a kiss on the lips.

"About these hostages," Trout said from about three feet beyond the door to the security room. He had a new flashlight that he was pointing at the doors up and down the hall.

"If I don't see you people inside in one minute, it's going to get rough."

There was no answer.

"Fifty seconds."

Nobody said anything.

At the end of a minute Trout picked up a chair he had brought with him from the security room. He lifted the chair high over his head and slammed it to the floor. The chair broke. It was wood, and splinters flew all around. After Trout smashed the chair, he kicked a couple of the larger pieces.

"That was a Giordano," he said.

Nothing.

"You know the Rembrandt that was by the front door here?"

Still nobody answered.

"In one more minute I'm going to cut it up into postage stamps. And then I'm going bowling with Alexander the Great's head."

Trout scooted another chair out of the security room.

"Twenty seconds."

The light came on, all the lights, including the row out front.

And shortly thereafter some keys sailed into the hallway

from a door down by the kitchen. The keys slid across the floor and banged into a wall.

"That's better," Trout said. "That's much better. It's almost perfect."

Quackenbush and his assistant stepped into the hallway with their hands on their heads.

"I didn't know you liked these old chairs so much," Trout said.

Trout unlocked the large front door. He led the guards outside and said, before anybody could congratulate him:

"We're in big trouble."

"Well, Christ," Finch said, looking around. "Where?"

Roebuck said he was starting to miss the police station.

Trout led the guards to the curb that ran around the naked-woman fountain, and sat down. The others joined him, including Lovely, who wanted his money for guarding the back door.

"It took fifteen minutes," Finch said. "The hundred was for the whole hour. You get twenty-five, minus withholding tax."

"Let's have it," Lovely said.

Trout looked up at everybody and said, "It's late."

Finch wanted to know if that was the big trouble Trout had mentioned previously.

Trout nodded.

"That's not big trouble," Finch said. "It's only mildly irritating."

Trout scooped up a bunch of gravel and shook it around in his hand like dice. "I don't want you to take this the wrong way," he said without looking at Finch, "but you've got to start thinking. I could use the help."

Finch said, "I'm *always* thinking." He was insulted.

"Think about how late it is."

"All right." Finch blinked five or six times.

"If we were in big trouble because it was late two minutes ago, what's the purpose of this seance?" Annabel wondered.

Trout said he was just trying to prove a point. This point was that you had to think ahead.

"We should have been almost loaded by the time you and Roebuck left the precinct," Trout said to Annabel, who nodded and closed her eyes.

"What held it up," Roebuck said, "was you got shot in the head and locked in, remember?"

"What happens if somebody finds out the precinct is empty before we get loaded?" Trout asked. "What if they come looking? They could come at any second."

Finch looked down the hill to the gate.

"We die," Roebuck said.

Trout tossed a pebble into the water at the base of the fountain. He said he might have come up with something that could buy them a little time:

"We go on strike."

Annabel opened her eyes.

Finch blinked some more.

Roebuck whistled.

"We, being the police."

Even the guards—who had been sitting with their heads down because they were depressed at having been caught—again—looked up.

"We go on strike," Roebuck said. "Yeah, hell, that ought to do it all right. That would explain why there were no police at the precinct. That ought to buy us a lot of time."

"Some," Trout said. "There's only one part of the strike idea that's a damn shame."

Finch, who was grinning, quit.

"It's a damn shame we can't go on strike from here." Trout turned to Annabel and Roebuck. "We ripped all the phone wires out."

Trout excused himself to use the bathroom inside the museum.

Finch doubted that he could take many more of these emotional ups and downs.

He sat down beside the guards and wondered for the first time if Trout had stolen this idea from an ex-con.

Roebuck said that if they had been going for a couple of hundred thousand apiece instead of a couple or three million, he'd have to think seriously about going to bed.

"When things start going bad," Quackenbush said, "there's sometimes no stopping them."

"It's settled," Annabel said. "We all go home and get jobs tomorrow morning."

Although some things hadn't gone exactly the way Trout had roughed them out on his various blackboards, it was awfully difficult to throw in the towel when there was no opponent, or even a *referee* around to catch it.

Get jobs?

It would be a little difficult to *get jobs* after having been millionaires, which was what they technically were, since the art was officially theirs.

Trout had no choice but to get in a squad car and drive it to the first pay phone and go on strike from there. That shouldn't take long.

"Right," Annabel said.

Trout got behind the wheel of the squad car that Annabel and Roebuck had arrived in. Annabel closed the door.

"While I'm gone, you can start dragging stuff into the hall."

Lovely had agreed to help move art to the door for a few hundred dollars more.

"Right," Annabel said. She had a list that showed what all the paintings were worth, and promised she wouldn't waste her time on anything that wasn't worth at least twenty grand; and she grinned.

Finch appeared at the front door carrying a large painting, which he held up for everybody to see. "I love this one of the bear eating two kids," he said.

It was a Degas.

"That's a shadow around two ballet dancers," Annabel told him.

"Oh," Finch said. "My mistake."

He carried the spectacular Degas back inside and leaned it against a wall near the front door.

Trout started the police car and drove off.

He found a pay phone rack a mile from the museum, stopped beside it, then got out. Miraculously the phone worked.

"Unbelievable," he said to himself.

That was the code word he should have requested from the Swiss bank when he flew there at great personal expense to open the numbered account. When you opened a numbered account, you got a number, a code word, and a free box of chocolates. Having the payoff for the artwork sent to a Swiss bank and then having it transferred a couple of times right into your lap beat running through fields with bags of ransom money as helicopters with ultraviolet cameras flew overhead. Trout had no idea why people bothered with ransom drops.

He shook himself back to the present and got the number of police headquarters from information.

He decided to go right to the top.

The more important officials were headquartered next door to a downtown precinct so that the chief or one of his assistants wouldn't be splattered with blood on the way to work. There was, however, a catwalk connecting the executive offices with the precinct in case anybody in power wanted to see how the criminals were doing.

Even though the administrative offices were closed at night, somebody was always on hand in case there was an emergency that required an executive decision.

Trout's call was answered after the fifth ring by a sleepy voice that belonged to a man named Boone.

"This is Bush over at the Thirty-third," Trout said. "And I need to talk to the chief, fast."

"We're asleep," Boone said.

"Put me through to him at home."

"Why?"

"It's an emergency."

"There's no such thing as an emergency at the Thirty-third," Boone said. "Tell me what your so-called emergency is and I'll call the chief and have him get back to you."

"It's personal," Trout said.

"The way it's supposed to work is that you give me the problem and I give it to the deputy chief, who makes a decision on who gets to sleep."

"Come on, you jackass."

"That does it," Boone said.

The chief of police was named Clark Grosvenor, and he wasn't upset in the least at being awakened from a sound sleep in the middle of the night. He had an obligation to the men who served under him. If one of them was in trouble, he wanted to be the first to hear about it.

Television would be the second to hear about it, then the newspapers, and so on.

Clark Grosvenor was thirty-eight. He was currently running the Mafia out of town, which wasn't making the already beleaguered people of New Jersey any too happy. He was also coming down hard on narcotics traffickers, which wasn't all that difficult because they were ubiquitous. So far he had sent several dozen narcotics traffickers off to prison, leaving, according to the head of the New Jersey or Bust Unit, only

2,875 to go. Clark Grosvenor's goal was to flush all the garbage across the state line so the city streets would be safe to walk on. This goal was not entirely civic-minded. Clark Grosvenor (how could "Grosvenor for Governor" possibly miss?) was going to have to walk the city streets himself campaigning.

Although quite a few veterans in the police department thought Clark Grosvenor was basically a horse's ass, he was generally regarded as a politician who could write his own ticket if he could only keep himself from being killed by one of the ten thousand paroled criminals currently roaming the streets.

Since it was just a month before he announced his candidacy, and because you never knew where positive publicity would come from, or when it might arrive, Grosvenor answered his phone.

"It's Boone downtown," the caller said.

"Hang on a second." Grosvenor turned on a lamp and put the call on a speaker. "Okay, what is it?"

"It's Bush from the Thirty-third."

"I thought you were Boone from downtown."

"Bush is on hold. He says he has an emergency he won't talk about with anyone but you."

"It's okay, put him on."

Grosvenor's wife, whose name was Charlotte, turned over and wondered why she hadn't unplugged the phone. She probably had. He had probably plugged it back in. Charlotte decided she was going to have to get some tools and remove the telephone wires from the wall.

"Go ahead," Boone told Trout.

"It's about time," Trout said.

The chief identified himself and asked what it was that couldn't wait until morning.

"It *is* morning," Trout said.

"Oh," Grosvenor said. "Right."

Trout told the chief that he and his men were upset about many of the working conditions at the Thirty-third.

"*What?*" the chief said.

"Hang up," Charlotte said, sitting up in bed.

"We want more money," Trout said.

The chief of police demanded to know what was going on.

"And new furniture. This place needs a paint job. Old, dark paint is bad for morale. We want something bright and happy."

"Now just one damn minute, my friend," Grosvenor said.

Charlotte turned on the bedside lamp.

"I want to see you in my office at eight A.M. sharp," Grosvenor said.

"If that's the way you feel about it, we're going on strike." Trout cleared his throat and said "By God," to prove he had meant what he said about the strike.

Grosvenor frowned.

Charlotte kicked her covers off and said that a strike was against the law. She gave her husband a disgusted look and stuck her feet over the side of the bed.

Trout demanded to know who had said that.

"I'm his wife," Charlotte said.

"Where's the chief?"

"We're right here," Charlotte said.

"I'm right here," Grosvenor said.

"A strike is against union rules and against the law," Charlotte told Trout.

"The hell with the union," Trout said. "The Mafia runs it. We'll strike the police department *and* the union."

"Strike the *union*," Grosvenor mumbled. "That's impossible."

Charlotte told Trout they would need to get back to him on this.

"I've got people driving five-year-old cars with bald tires

and no reverse gears. Who gets back to the officer who suffers spinal damage because of a rotten transmission?"

"Me," Grosvenor said. "I'll get back to him. What hospital is he in?"

"Plus we want one more homosexual. We've got an odd number, and they're fighting like crazy."

Charlotte got out of bed and walked around to the speaker box. "We need more time."

Trout told them he had more demands and would call back.

The chief said, "Let's talk about this over a cup of coffee in a couple of hours. And *I'm* buying." Grosvenor smiled even though nobody was looking at him.

The line went dead.

Trout got back in his squad car and pointed it toward the museum.

He didn't feel the need to speed.

At the Grosvenor apartment Charlotte said:

"This is *exactly* what you get for answering the telephone."

She reminded her husband that they were not in the market for *bad* publicity, and that this was not the time to alienate a sizable cross section of the voting public.

"I'll have somebody's ass for this," Grosvenor said. "Alienate who?"

"People who don't want to be run over by police cars with no brakes."

Clark Grosvenor got an electric razor from the bathroom and shaved as he selected a navy three-piece suit from his closet. He said his administration would not be intimidated.

"What are you doing?" Charlotte asked.

Grosvenor put his electric razor down and said he was getting dressed. He said this was called rolling up your sleeves and watching out for the public's interest.

"Then for God's sake roll your sleeves up."

138

Grosvenor looked at his sleeves, which had French cuffs, and he *pushed* each one up an inch.

"Take that damn vest off. It's almost time for breakfast."

"I will not."

Grosvenor tied his tie and called Boone downtown and asked for a car to be sent around immediately.

He looked in a mirror. He was *beautiful.*

Charlotte selected from her closet something much more casual—jeans and a beige blouse. "What we need the month before you announce your candidacy is the public's confidence, its sympathy, not its company."

"Maybe one of those striking bastards will shoot me," Grosvenor said.

Charlotte accepted that statement as a viable alternative, not as sarcasm.

She would have run for governor herself had she not been busy with the Junior League and its various charity balls. The League had been out of creative charities to sponsor and was about to go with a Thanksgiving ball for Native American salmon fishermen when Charlotte was called in to bail them out.

"If this looks as bad as it sounds, we need to drop it on somebody as soon as we can," she said, pulling on some sneakers.

"Where are you going?" Grosvenor asked as he buttoned his vest.

"With you," Charlotte answered. "Don't forget, I'm a stockholder."

All appeared to be in order when Trout got back to the museum.

He told Annabel how well the strike had gone. When he finished explaining what he had said, he wiped a drop of blood from his temple; it kept him from feeling too over-confident.

"What about here?" he asked.

"It's going fine, except for the conversation."

Just then Roebuck stepped outside with a head under his right arm. It was a bust of Alexander the Great. Roebuck carried the bust as though it were a football. "This guy didn't want to come along peacefully," he said, grinning.

Finch stacked two large paintings along a front wall and wanted to know if the artists, Rembrandt and Ysenbrandt, were relatives. He then said this one guy named Duck could really "draw."

"See what I mean?" Annabel said.

A couple of dozen works of art had already been relocated in the front hallway. Most were large. Somebody had stuffed *Man's Inner Struggles* in a garbage can.

Trout brought Finch and Roebuck up to date on the strike, and while they were all together on the front steps, he waved for Lovely to join them.

Lovely, who still had a stomach ache and wanted his money so he could leave, had been sitting on a bench by the naked woman out front. He shuffled over and was thanked sincerely for all his help.

"The profit is going to the shrinks," Lovely said. "I'll wind up in the hole."

Trout removed from a back pocket the envelope containing Lovely's original fee of one thousand dollars. Trout carried the envelope inside the museum and paused before a piece of furniture that was lavishly carved and painted. He opened a drawer on the front of the piece of furniture and tossed the envelope into a brightly colored pan. He closed the drawer and said that, as far as he was concerned, everybody was even.

"Are you talking to me?" Lovely asked.

"It's worth what, four thousand?"

"More," Quackenbush said.

"For a job fairly well done," Trout said, extending his hand to Lovely.

Lovely shook Trout's hand limply. "What is that thing?"

"A commode," Trout said. "It's an antique French commode."

"You talk about getting your just deserts," Annabel said, smiling.

"A *what?*"

"Commode. It was made by a master craftsman in seventeen what?"

"Sixty-six," Quackenbush said.

Finch said, "It's where you . . ."

"I know what a commode is," Lovely said.

"But it doesn't look like it," Trout said.

"You could tell everybody it's an icebox," Roebuck suggested.

"Everybody *who?*"

"Your friends," Roebuck said.

"Tell my friends it's an icebox." Lovely stared at his antique.

"You could almost play poker on it," Roebuck said, honestly trying to help. "And never have to take a break."

Lovely picked up the antique French commode that was hand carved by a master craftsman in 1766. "This is heavier than it looks."

He took a couple of steps in the direction of the front gates.

"Say," he said to Quackenbush. "You think this place would be interested in buying this thing back?"

Quackenbush said he didn't doubt it.

"How much?"

"Fifteen percent. Seven or eight hundred."

"So how do I do it?"

"Call."

"Who?"

"The *new* director of security."

Lovely lifted the French commode and carried it a few more yards.

"I hate to keep bringing this up," Finch said, "but nobody is going to be able to call anybody around here because of the wires I ripped out."

Quackenbush said he'd get the phones fixed in the morning."

"Say." Lovely stopped to catch his breath. "How long are you people going to be here?"

"Not long," Trout answered.

"You think I might get a lift?"

"Sure."

"For a price," Finch said.

Lovely moved his antique onto the grass, sat on top of it, and crossed his legs.

"I'll get the truck and back it up to the door," Trout said.

The others said they'd keep shifting the artwork up front.

Trout walked a few yards toward the trucks, stopped, cleared his throat, and said that all he needed now was the keys. He trotted to Lovely and got both sets. He held them up and waved them at the group still gathered on the steps.

"Got them," he said.

"Hey," Finch said. "What if he would have gone home with the keys?"

Trout grinned and said there was no use crying over unopened milk, and he walked with a spring in his step to the trucks in the gravel parking lot around the corner.

Trout hoisted himself onto the back bumper of the truck nearest the museum, since it was the handiest, and put a key in the lock.

He stood there, with one hand around the door handle and the other around the key, for about fifteen seconds.

It seemed longer, though. It seemed like hours.

Trout stared at the lock and key and then jumped backwards off the bumper. He stumbled around but somehow managed to keep his balance even though he bumped against a bush.

He grabbed the bush and straightened himself up.

He opened his mouth and started to call out for help but decided there might not be any reason to panic just yet. So he walked to the other truck and climbed onto that one exactly as he had done with the first, but his grip wasn't as strong this time and he hung a few feet above the ground for only a couple of seconds. His hands were wet.

Trout jumped off this truck without even having messed around with the lock or the key.

He sat down on a plant. He sat there until he almost started crying. He bit his bottom lip and told himself that weeping wouldn't accomplish anything. He talked himself out of being sad and was actually angry by the time he returned to the truck parked nearest the museum.

Trout opened the driver's door and crawled inside and looked under the seat. He also felt in the crack where the seat and backrest came together. He opened and closed the glove compartment. He sat behind the wheel and then in the passenger seat.

He looked at himself in the rear-view mirror and said, "It's going to be okay."

He smiled at himself.

He found himself almost deranged.

He looked around the front of the truck once more.

He got out and slammed the door.

He slammed it so hard the whole truck vibrated.

"What was that?" Annabel asked from just inside the front hallway.

"Trout getting in the truck," Finch guessed.

They kept dragging heavy art to the hall.

Trout got in the other truck and did the same thing—he inspected every inch of the cab—and then he got out, slam-

143

ming the door even harder, and walked around both trucks half a dozen times.

He wondered what he was doing here. He was no criminal. He should have been dealing three-card monte to tourists in the park.

He looked carefully at the front of both trucks, and the back, and the sides.

He even got down and looked underneath the trucks, searching, perhaps, for a piece of Finch's jump suit from when he dropped his high school graduation ring a long, long time ago.

"There, damn it," Trout said, wiping his hands on his shirt after he had crawled around underneath both trucks. "That's that."

He had done everything possible in a reasonably calm and orderly manner.

Then he started crying.

It was the best he had felt all night.

When Annabel heard the strange sound, which was Trout crying, she stepped outside and listened.

She walked to the edge of the building and peeked around.

Finch and Roebuck locked the guards in a closet and followed Annabel.

Trout was wiping his face with his shirttail when she stuck her head around the side of the building.

"Hi," she said.

"Hi," Trout said. He tucked his shirt in. "How's it going?"

"Pretty good," Annabel said. "Pretty good."

Finch guessed that Trout was having a relapse. He told Trout to have a seat inside somewhere and let him back the truck up to the front door.

"He's turned white," Roebuck said quietly.

The three of them joined Trout by the trucks.

Both sets of keys were at Trout's feet. He noticed all three of his friends looking at the keys, so he picked them up.

"How do you feel?" Finch asked.

"Not so good, actually," Trout said.

His eyes were glassy.

"I feel fair."

"Toss me the keys," Finch said.

Trout straightened up and said, "Get back."

Finch stopped and glanced at Roebuck, who was glancing at Annabel, who was frowning at Trout.

Trout pitched both sets of keys a couple of inches in the air three or four times. "Let's go over here," he said. He walked from the gravel parking lot to the soft ground underneath some lovely mimosa trees.

"He's out of his head," Finch whispered. "It's time for Roebuck to grab him."

Annabel told Finch to be quiet.

They followed Trout to the trees, where he leaned against a trunk and stared at the keys.

"There's no easy way to put this."

"Put what?" Finch asked.

Trout looked at his three friends, bless their hearts, and decided that there *had* to be some way to spare them the pain he had just experienced.

"About the trucks," Trout said.

Trout looked at them.

So did the others.

The trucks were about thirty yards off, facing their way.

"When we got here, things got a little confused. First of all, Lovely pulled them in front-first, so I had him back them in. All the bumpers are scratched about the same from when we came in through the front gates. You know what's the most pathetic thing about this?"

"About what?" Finch asked.

"You remember that candy bar? You remember that Butterfinger wrapper from the candy bar you had on the way to the police station?"

"It was good. It gives you energy."

"If we'd left the damn wrapper on the seat we'd be okay."

Finch took the Butterfinger wrapper out of his pocket and looked at it.

"This is the worst luck in the history of the civilized world," Trout said. "And maybe since longer than that."

"There's one bite left. You can have it."

"I don't know which truck is empty," Trout said.

Annabel was the only one to react; she pulled her head back a couple of inches as though a bee had flown in front of her face.

Trout said in an even tone that both cabs were clean, and he repeated the part about how the front fenders were similarly scratched. "And, of course, they're both the same make, the same color, the same everything."

"Come on, Trout, it's late," Finch said. "Which truck are the police in?"

"I don't know. You don't know. Nobody knows."

Annabel simply sat down on the grass.

Finch looked at her. He looked at the two trucks, which seemed for the first time to be so similar, it was almost comical. The trucks had never been parked side by side. For a second Finch thought he was having double vision. Then he looked at the last bite of his Butterfinger candy bar, which he ate.

"Which truck are the police in?" Finch asked again. "Which truck is empty?"

"How many times do I have to tell you? I *don't* know."

Roebuck walked around behind Annabel and massaged her neck and shoulders.

Finch knelt down and asked Annabel if *she* knew which

146

truck the police were in; Finch said that he needed to know because they had guns in there with them, guns and dynamite and there was no telling what else, remember?

Annabel didn't answer.

Trout turned and walked toward the museum.

Finch couldn't *believe* nobody would talk to him, so he picked up a branch from a small tree Lovely had uprooted, and he threw the branch at Trout, missing him by about three feet to the right.

"Stop that," Trout said.

Finch threw another limb. Trout jumped to get out of the way. He trotted to his left and ducked in behind a fender as a large dirt clod broke against the windshield of the truck nearest the museum.

"You've cost us *millions*," Finch screamed.

"I'm the one who got us the millions in the first place," Trout shouted.

"You goddamn *Indian giver*," Finch yelled.

The mood in the back of one of the identical white vans was almost downright festive.

"There's still some yelling," one of the officers said.

Three or four people were at the doors, listening.

Lieutenant Bush had to turn Pike's lighter on several times to get them to calm down, and to get their attention.

"They're coming apart," Buck said. He grabbed his neck with his right hand and made a choking motion. "They're trying to kill each other."

"Be quiet," Lieutenant Bush whispered.

He crept to the front of the truck and brought all those who had not had front-row seats up to date. First, he had them all take off their shoes. He told them what he and Buck and Sergeant House had overheard, and what he had concluded because of it:

1. There were two trucks; the other truck was identical to the one they were in.
2. They were obviously at a place that contained valuables, a bank or something like that.
3. Their captors didn't know which truck was empty, and therefore couldn't open *either* one for a look.
4. So they probably weren't exactly kidnapped, at least not for ransom, at least not yet.
   "Being stolen is worse than being kidnapped," Buck said.
5. Because of the lateness of the hour, their captors would undoubtedly try to determine which truck was which by listening.
6. They had to be very quiet from now on.

After Lieutenant Bush had whispered all this to the others, Officer Mounds, who was getting chilly standing around in his undershorts, reported that something had just crashed against the side of the truck—a rock, he guessed.

Lieutenant Bush assured the others that their goal was no longer simply to stay alive. Things did seem to be deteriorating by the second out there. When the next opportunity presented itself, the police would become the aggressors; there was no doubt about that. Lieutenant Bush's new plan was to remain calm and listen for further signs of vulnerability.

"That sounds a lot like the old plan," Buck said.

"If it hadn't been for lard-butt, none of this would have happened," Billows said. "My God, falling for a story about a leather chair."

Sergeant House wanted to know what he was supposed to do—shoot everybody who walked in off the street?

"You're supposed to lose a hundred pounds so finding a comfortable place to sit won't dominate your life," Billows said.

"It's getting quiet out there," Buck said.

"Maybe they've murdered each other," Mounds guessed.

"Sorry," Finch said.

Trout told him he could have put an eye out. *Again.*

They sat on the curb by the fountain out front and tried to think of a way to figure out which truck was full, which was potentially more dangerous than figuring out which truck was empty; but it seemed to make more sense.

Trout had just returned from another walk around both trucks. He had tried to smell cherry-vodka fumes this time.

"Why the hell didn't you spill some?" Trout asked Lovely.

"You'll have to forgive me. I'm just too neat."

They were in such desperate shape, they had invited Lovely over for his thoughts. He was feeling a tiny bit better.

As Trout concentrated, he drew in the dirt with a stick.

He kept looking at his watch.

After they had thought for three minutes, Trout started looking at his watch every fifteen seconds, and that depressed him so much he could barely stand it.

"We could always shoot the damn trucks," Finch said.

They were trying so hard to get along, Trout didn't comment on Finch's idea. He wanted to, though. He wanted to roll around in the leaves and laugh. Shoot the trucks? God help us, Trout thought. No, on second thought, forget it. This would only depress God.

Roebuck bailed Trout out.

"Then they could shoot us back through the same holes," he said. "That is, if bullets would go through the side of the truck in the first place."

Trout gave Roebuck a thank-you-so-much look.

Finch shrugged and said he was only trying to help.

"I might have a little something," Lovely said.

Everybody looked up at him. He was sitting on his antique French commode.

"Is it better than shooting the trucks?" Trout asked.

"Oh, *yeah.*"

"I don't see the purpose of that question," Finch said.

"It's a thousand times better."

"Nothing is a thousand times better."

"You want to bet?"

Lovely hopped off his antique and said he didn't want to be greedy or anything. "But I would sure feel better about this if I didn't get shut out. If I came up with the key to this thing and everybody got their millions, you would think I deserved some kind of finder's fee."

"We could always torture it out of you," Finch said.

"If it's good—if it's a good idea and you say it fast—we'll take care of you," Trout said.

"How about this? How about you give me a little something first? Then I give you my idea. If it's lousy, I'll give back what you gave me."

Trout decided that anything was better than sitting around some more, ducking dawn, so he scratched Lovely an IOU for five hundred dollars using the inside cover of some of Annabel's matches. He signed and dated the contract.

"Somehow this doesn't fill me with confidence," Lovely said, accepting the matches. He put them in his top drawer. "This IOU isn't for more furniture, it's for currency."

Trout nodded.

"The key is weight," Lovely said.

"Give it back," Finch said. He had already checked the shocks and springs of both trucks. Both vans were the same approximate distance above ground.

"Here's what you do," Lovely said. "You make a couple of tires go flat. At the same time. The tire that goes flat first is the truck with the police in it because of the weight."

Roebuck said that all things considered, that wasn't bad.

"I should have thought of that," Trout said.

Trout got down on his knees so he could see. He held his right hand up, palm out.

"Do it exactly together, when I say *now*," Trout said.

"Okay," Roebuck said.

"Okay," Finch said. "Say one, two, three, *now*."

Finch and Roebuck had sticks and they were going to let the air out of the rear left tires on the trucks simultaneously.

"Excuse me," Annabel said. She was behind Trout. "Has anybody got any cigarettes?"

Trout waved Annabel away, counted to three, and said, "*Now*."

Finch and Roebuck stuck their sticks into their respective air spouts.

Trout stood up.

A lot of air was coming out of Finch's tire, so much, in fact, he had to duck out of the way.

"Slow down," Trout said.

"I can't," Finch said, wrestling with his stick and air spout. "It's stuck. It's stuck *bad*."

The air rushing out of Finch's tire kicked up some dust.

The four of them stood together and watched the tire on the right-hand truck go flat in about twenty seconds.

"Maybe that's why you didn't think of it," Roebuck said. "It stinks."

"Get the damn jack," Trout said.

Lovely gave Annabel her matches back and helped change the flat.

"It's a good thing the spare wasn't locked in the back," Finch said, trying to be pleasant.

After they got the tire changed, they returned to the

front of the museum and sat by the statue, which they were getting a little sick of.

Trout went inside to throw some cold water on his face and came back in a slightly better mood. He could sense that his friends were about ready to strap what art they could on their backs and head for the hills, like pack mules.

He passed around some paper cups full of water and said rather confidently that there was *still* no need to panic.

"Why?" Finch asked.

Trout gave him a dirty look.

Finch stretched.

"What we need to do now," Trout said, "is something that makes absolutely *perfect* sense."

Roebuck yawned.

Lovely yawned.

Trout almost yawned.

"Stop it," he said.

Finch poured some water onto his right palm and rubbed his eyes.

"The one thing that's open for sure at this time of night where we might get some help is a hospital," Trout said. "Roebuck, you and Finch get in one of the squad cars and go to the hospital that's south of here over by the park and see if you can find something useful."

"Like what?" Finch asked.

"Like some cigarettes," Annabel said.

Trout said he didn't know. "Have a look around. Maybe you can get some kind of portable X-ray machine that we can try on the trucks, or some kind of tiny drill."

"Okay," Roebuck said.

This wasn't too bad, so everybody quit yawning.

"Now, if you see a truck on the way, a semi big enough to get the art inside, something that's got a covered back like the ones we have, steal it. Don't waste any time looking all over the place, though. Go to the hospital and come back, and if you see a truck parked along the way or close by on a side street, check it out."

"I need a lift," Lovely said. "I live south."

"Sure thing," Finch said.

"I'm out of cigarettes," Annabel said. "I've only got two left."

"What kind?" Roebuck asked.

"Nonfilters. Get me three or four packs."

Roebuck said he didn't have that much change.

"Do you people *mind?*" Trout asked.

Finch said they minded real good. "What we're doing now is rolling over and playing dead."

"He's just kidding," Roebuck said, getting up. "This has got a chance."

Trout said he wanted them back from the hospital, if they didn't see any trucks to steal, within forty-five minutes. "While you're gone, we'll keep trying to figure out which truck is which."

At the mention of the truck problem Roebuck sat back down and hung his head with the rest of them.

"Listen," Trout said. "We're still right in the middle of this thing. If worse comes to worst, we can just guess at a truck and open it."

"That's fifty-fifty odds," Finch said.

Trout said he had heard a lot worse.

"Yeah, but before we started this," Finch said, looking up, "you said the odds were a *thousand* to one in our favor."

"Well," Trout said, smiling and trying to be very upbeat, "we lost the home-field advantage. And at least if we lose, we don't have to pay a bookie his commission."

"No, we'll pay the lawyers instead," Finch said.

Trout helped everybody up and assisted Lovely with the French commode. It barely fit in the backseat of the squad car. Two legs stuck out of a rear window.

Finch apologized for not reacting more positively to

Trout's pep talk. Looking for trucks to steal on the way to a hospital full of all kinds of gadgets was fundamentally sound. Finch said he was simply tired, hungry, frightened, sleepy, and nervous. He promised Trout they would return in less than forty-five minutes with something of great value.

They checked their watches and determined that it was around nine of, two of, five after, or ten after—three in the morning.

They rounded it off to three, straight up.

Five

Grosvenor got out of the unmarked car, which was driven by a detective named Moon, and looked up at the front doors of the Thirty-third Precinct.

It was dark up there.

"This is inexcusable," Grosvenor said.

"Let's get the mayor in on this," Charlotte said. "We don't need to be in charge of what's going on here for even five more minutes."

Grosvenor was met on the steps by one of his assistants, whose name was Rick. Rick also wore a three-piece suit and was a shorter version of the man he worked for.

Charlotte thought the two of them looked as though they had just come from the opera.

"What's going on here?" Rick asked, looking at Detective Moon, who was a rumpled-up older fellow.

"It looks to me like we've driven even the police over to New Jersey," Moon said.

"It's a possible strike," Grosvenor said.

"Strike?" Rick looked up at the darkened building. "What would these people hold out for, new canasta cards?"

The chief walked up the steps and attempted to open the front door. "It's locked," he said to those waiting on the sidewalk. "Somebody get this door open."

Nobody on the sidewalk moved or spoke.

"Give me a key to this door," the chief said.

Rick told him he didn't have one.

"Who *does?*"

"I don't know."

"You're telling me I don't have a key to one of my own precincts?"

"There's one downtown somewhere," Rick said.

Grosvenor tried to force the doors open, and when that didn't work, he opened his suit coat and removed his pistol.

Detective Moon told the chief not to smash the glass door too low. "Hit it high so nothing will fall and open a vein in your wrist."

"Call the mayor," Charlotte said.

Rick told her he was in the Bahamas.

The chief smashed the glass in and jumped back. When the glass had settled, Grosvenor stepped inside the Thirty-third Precinct. Presently he stepped back outside. "Where's the light switch?"

Detective Moon went to the car for a flashlight.

"He's been like this for weeks," Rick whispered to Charlotte. "Some days he walks around at noon, looking for trouble. He wants to be visible."

"If he keeps this up, he'll be visible, all right. Lying in state."

Rick took the flashlight from Detective Moon and went up the front steps two at a time. "Clark, we need to go slow on this. We need to take our time. We can't afford the big screw-up."

"What is there to screw up?"

"We don't even want to know."

Grosvenor turned the flashlight on and entered the Thirty-third Precinct once more. He found the switch and turned the overhead lights on. He and Rick and Detective Moon walked across the wooden floors toward the abandoned reception desk.

Charlotte waited at the door in case anybody with a camera showed up.

The chief asked Moon what he thought of the situation.

"If any of these people have quit or anything like that, I'd sure like a transfer here."

Grosvenor got on the phone at the front desk and called the precinct to the south. He requested that half a dozen officers be sent to the Thirty-third at once.

"Listen," Moon said as Grosvenor hung up.

Detective Moon got down on his hands and knees and put his right ear to the floor.

"I thought I heard something," he said.

"What?" Rick asked.

"I could be wrong," Moon said, standing up, "but it sounded like wild animals howling."

The first truck Finch and Roebuck spotted was across from an apartment building that was made out of glass and aluminum. The building was eight or ten stories tall, and it faced the parking lot on which the truck sat.

This truck wasn't as large as what they had been used to, but Roebuck supposed it might do in a pinch, so he swung the police car into the lot and killed the engine.

"What if it's full of stuff?" Finch wondered.

Roebuck doubted that anybody would park a truck full of anything valuable in an obscure parking lot. "Even if it has something in the back, we can throw it out at the museum."

"Who said valuable?" Finch said. "It's probably full of snakes."

Lovely asked how much farther south they were going; he was trying to decide if he should get out before there was any more trouble.

The reason nobody hopped out of the police car to steal the truck, which was about half as long as the vans they had rented, was because they didn't know how.

"We should have brought along a coat hanger," Finch said, looking in the glove compartment for something useful.

"How come?" Roebuck wondered.

"So my jacket won't get wrinkled."

"There's no need to be a wise-ass."

About all Finch knew about car theft was what he'd seen in the late movies on television. People usually stuck something between the glass and rubber part of the window, or they picked the lock. Then they leaned under the dashboard and hooked a couple of wires together.

"Yeah, the ignition wires," Roebuck said. He had a nephew who stole cars, and seemed to remember the trick was touching the two ignition wires together.

"Call your nephew."

"He's dead."

"Well, that's pleasant."

"I wasn't going to mention it, until you got specific," Roebuck said, checking the time. They had wasted a minute and twenty seconds. "Come on, let's get on with it."

"With *what?*"

Lovely, who was getting nervous, asked them to help him get the antique French commode off his lap.

Finch ignored Lovely. He got out of the squad car. He peeked in through the driver's window of the truck and saw nothing of consequence.

"Before you start swinging, try the door, it might be unlocked," Roebuck said.

"I never even thought of that."

"You're tired."

The alarm didn't begin ringing when Finch grabbed the door handle. Nothing happened when he did that. The alarm started ringing when Finch pushed the button on the handle and yanked.

The alarm was shrill.

"Now you've gone and done it," Roebuck said, starting the police car.

"What's going on?" Lovely asked. He was trying to get out of the backseat by crawling underneath the French antique, which was stuck in the door.

The alarm that rang from inside the truck wasn't all that loud. At noon you probably wouldn't even notice it. But in the middle of the night the alarm served its purpose and frightened everybody.

Finch yanked his hand away as though he had been electrocuted. He stumbled backwards and was almost run over by Roebuck, who had swung open the passenger door on the police car. Finch dove in headfirst. Roebuck gunned the motor and drove over a curb.

Lovely, trapped under the French commode, rode several blocks with his head outside the car.

Trout stuck a broom handle into the gas tank on the side of one of the trucks. The handle went in several feet, got stuck, and Trout had to really shove to get it going again.

"When we picked up the trucks," he said over his shoulder, "both gas tanks were full. Even though the needles on the dashboard gauges are about the same, the truck full of people had to burn a little more gas because of the extra weight, right?"

Trout shoved the broom handle several more inches into the gas tank.

"I said, right?"

"What?" Annabel said.

She had walked a few yards toward the front gates. She was feeling around in some tall grass for a cigarette butt she had discarded a few minutes ago.

"The truck with the police in back should have burned more gas. Because of the extra weight. Isn't that the way it works?"

"I have no idea," Annabel said, feeling through the grass.

"That's *exactly* the way it works."

"Congratulations."

"So I'll measure here, and if one tank has even a tiny bit less gas in it, that's the one."

Annabel found a butt with about a quarter of an inch of tobacco on it and fired it up, almost burning her nose. She stood up and looked at Trout.

"If the first truck you measure has the *most* gas left, then you won't know that, will you, because the second mark on the broom handle will be below the first. In fact, the second mark probably won't even show up."

"I'll use *two* broom handles that are the exact same size."

"Fair enough," Annabel said, taking one last half-puff on the cigarette butt.

Trout tried to shove the broom handle down to where the gas was, but it got stuck again. He tried to work the handle free by pulling it toward him, but it snapped about in half.

"Damn," Trout said.

He put the gas cap on the tank and scratched his back with his half of the broom handle.

When Grosvenor turned on the light in the room where the holding cell was, people started screaming.

Mrs. Emerson screamed first.

Her scream was high-pitched and sounded like something out of *Carmen*.

A couple of the other women, who had their gowns hiked above their knees and had been using their furs for pillows, also screamed.

Mrs. Emerson's outburst caused Chief Grosvenor to draw his pistol, which caused a couple of the men to scream along with the women.

Even Detective Moon screamed a little and drew his weapon.

One of the women collapsed into a man's arms, and the screaming stopped.

"Put your hands up," the chief of police said.

"Go ahead, kill us," Charles Emerson called over his shoulder as he knelt to attend to the woman who had almost passed out.

Grosvenor approached the holding cell cautiously. He told everybody to move away from the bars and sit on the bunks. He looked at their nice clothes and asked what they had been charged with.

"Loitering," Charles Emerson said. "We were charged with loitering while we were reporting a crime."

"We weren't booked," a man in a tux said. "We were herded."

"Like common thugs." Charles Emerson handed his mother a handkerchief and turned to point at Grosvenor. "I know who you are. You're the chief of police."

Charlotte whispered into her husband's ear, "Put your gun away."

He did that.

"Excuse me," Rick said, stepping between the chief and the people in the holding cell. "We just got here. You're going to have to tell us what happened. Did you come here of your own volition?"

"We were robbed," Charles Emerson said, approaching the bars.

Grosvenor frowned and took a step back.

"My mother and some other women had their purses stolen."

"This makes no sense," Grosvenor said.

"Tell them you have to go," Charlotte whispered.

"Never."

"Your purses were snatched?" Rick moved nearer the bars.

"That's correct." Charles Emerson straightened his tie. "We were at a party a block and a half away, a fund raiser, where my mother had just pledged a hundred and fifty thousand dollars to a shelter for the insane."

"You walked here?"

"Correct."

"When?" Rick was taking notes.

"Around midnight."

"Then what happened?"

"We tried to report the crime to a large man at the front desk."

"He was an ape," one of the women said.

"He had hands the size of Ping-pong paddles," one of the men added.

Charles Emerson nodded. "We were told to fill out forms not *five* minutes after the criminals who had stolen our purses disappeared into the shadows. They ran right by the front door, as a matter of fact."

"Forms are policy," Grosvenor said.

"And *then*," Charles Emerson said, grabbing onto a couple of bars, "they brought us here at gunpoint and turned off the lights and heat."

"You're certain they were *policemen?*" Rick asked.

"Of course."

"I kept thinking they would come back and spray something on us," Mrs. Emerson said.

Charles Emerson demanded that his party be released, this second, and he shook his finger at the chief again.

"First things first," Grosvenor said.

"Like *what?*"

"A key."

The second truck that Finch and Roebuck found was parked on a side street about three blocks from the hospital.

Roebuck saw the truck out of the corner of his eye and backed the police car next to it.

There was a dog in the truck. It was yellow. It had its nose near the window. It barked once.

"What was that?" Lovely asked. He was hiding on the floorboard.

"Go," Finch said.

"Wait, it quit."

Roebuck opened his door for a closer look at the yellow dog, which had started panting. "It quit barking."

"You can't bark and bite at the same time," Finch said.

Roebuck said that this dog looked friendly. He tapped on the truck window and the dog took a step back.

"Now it's stretched out on the seat. You're not going to believe this. The keys are in the ignition."

"Somebody give me a gun," Lovely said. "So I can defend myself."

Finch got out, looked around, and joined Roebuck at the driver's window. The dog was on the floorboard, trying to crawl under the front seat.

"He's a real sweetheart," Roebuck said.

"Maybe he's rabid."

Roebuck said that what he was going to do now was remove the window. Finch stepped way back. Roebuck put both hands on the glass and pushed with all his might. The window didn't break. It wrinkled up and bent down by the bottom. Roebuck pushed the window on into the front seat. "These things are about five percent glass and the rest plastic," Roebuck said, unlocking the door from the inside.

163

"Nice dog," Finch said.

The yellow dog seemed to agree and it rolled over onto its back on the floorboard.

Roebuck got behind the wheel, scratched the dog on its stomach, and told Finch to follow him back to the museum.

Finch nodded.

Just then somebody standing in the doorway of a building shouted:

"*Say.*"

Finch stood with his back exposed.

Roebuck looked around Finch and reported that all he could see was the shadow of a person who appeared to be holding something long and skinny.

"Start the truck and go," Finch whispered.

"What about the police car?" Roebuck whispered back.

"You're right. Shoot whoever it is, instead."

"Say," the shadow in the doorway said again. "*Thanks!*"

"Don't shoot him yet," Finch said.

Detective Moon had found some welding equipment in the property room, which had been left unlocked, and he was trying to blast or melt open the lock on the door of the holding cell. He wasn't too good at it, though, and sparks were flying all over the place.

Rick returned from upstairs with a printout. He said there were no complaints showing up on any of the computers, and while dodging sparks, he told Grosvenor what he had learned about the people in the cell. "One of them has a record."

Grosvenor nodded.

"In a way. One of them has a record *company*. He owns it."

"That's not funny," Grosvenor said.

"This is a disaster," Charlotte said. "It's catastrophic. Your officers are on strike. They're demanding more homosexuals and cars that run, and now *this*."

"And your point is?" Grosvenor had about decided there was no good publicity around here.

"My point is that we need to think of a way out of this mess before you get fired."

Grosvenor wadded the printout into a ball and pitched it into a garbage can.

"How about this?" Charlotte said to Rick more than anybody else. "We pay those people a little something to keep their mouths shut."

Rick looked at the people in evening clothes and said it didn't look to him as if they would be all that impressed by an offer of money.

"I'm not bribing anybody," Grosvenor said.

Detective Moon stopped blasting and lifted his welding hood. He walked over to where the chief and his people were standing, and said that he had just burned his neck. He tilted his head to the right to show everybody the burn. "I need a workmen's comp form."

"Get back there and cut those people out," Grosvenor said.

"I don't think that's a very good idea. Two or more of them are lawyers."

Now that the sparks had stopped, one of the men in tuxedos waved at Grosvenor, who had no choice but to see what he wanted.

"My name is Howard Young," the man said. "I'm an attorney."

"So am I," Grosvenor said, "although I don't practice. Obviously."

"Good," Howard Young said. "I mean, good you're an attorney, not good that you aren't practicing."

The two men smiled at each other.

"I didn't have much light to work with," Howard Young said, holding out a piece of paper. "And it was so cold, my hand got numb. But this is a rough approximation of our lawsuit. The 'AD' in the left-hand margin stands for assault with a deadly weapon. The rest of it ought to be self-explanatory."

Howard Young rejoined his wife on a bench.

Detective Moon turned his torch on the cell lock again.

Grosvenor reported to his wife and his assistant that he and the city had just been sued for eleven million dollars, and he went to the fountain for a drink of water.

"You're sitting better than the rest of us," Rick said quietly. "You can always divorce him."

Rick relieved Detective Moon, who had burned a hole in his shirt sleeve.

"We could always *kidnap* them until this blows over," Grosvenor said, nodding toward the cell. His color was bad.

"That would never work," Charlotte said.

Grosvenor admitted he'd been afraid of that.

"But you're in the right ball park."

Finch and Roebuck had forgotten they were the police, but they were quickly reminded by the man who had called out from the apartment doorway. His name was Stottlemeyer.

"Thank God for you men," Stottlemeyer said, shuffling across the street. He wore a robe and carried a rifle, for which he had a permit, which he had in his robe pocket. He shook hands with Finch and Roebuck and called the dog, who jumped across Roebuck's lap and landed on the street.

Stottlemeyer asked Roebuck if he had found any evidence in the truck.

"Evidence?" Roebuck said.

"Which way did he go?"

"He?" Finch said.

"You're telling me it was a *woman* that tried to steal my truck? Not that it would surprise me. Nothing surprises me, except you men getting here so quick."

166

"He went up there," Finch said, pointing straight ahead.

"You can track him down," Stottlemeyer said, resting his rifle on the hood.

Roebuck told him he shouldn't leave his key in the ignition.

"That's what you think. Try the key. It's my wife's brother's invention. Try it and tell me what you think."

Roebuck tried to start the truck, but the key wouldn't turn.

"It fits the slot, is all," Stottlemeyer said. "The theory is that a thief is either going to get caught sitting here trying to start the truck or he's going to get mad and go home. My wife's brother says he's going to get a patent on this thing. Can you imagine that? A key that doesn't work. I keep telling him the way you make money is with things that work, not with things that don't."

Roebuck tried the key a couple more times, then handed it to Stottlemeyer.

"Are you kidding? Put it back."

The yellow dog was even harder to understand than the key that didn't turn in the ignition.

Roebuck climbed out of the truck and listened with Finch as Stottlemeyer showed off one of the city's most unusual watchdogs.

The yellow dog crept into the street a few steps, where he froze. He looked at the three men and then retraced his steps—it was like film being run backwards—and disappeared behind the truck.

"Hey, come here, you," Stottlemeyer said to the dog, which didn't. He whined from his hiding place behind the truck. "That dog has roots in vaudeville."

"It looks to me like it's got roots in its head," Roebuck said.

Stottlemeyer explained that this dog, whose name was Henry, barked all the time. "Sometimes he even barks in his sleep."

"Henry is a person's name," Finch said. "No wonder he's not all there."

Roebuck said not necessarily; there was a chicken hawk named Henry in some comic book he'd read a long time ago.

Stottlemeyer said that the dog was also his wife's brother's. "The dog barks all the time, right?"

Finch said he guessed so.

"*Except* when it's got a reason to bark. Then it gets quiet. You see the point? As long as the dog is barking, there's nothing to worry about. The second it *quits* barking, that means there's some truck thieves around."

"A key that doesn't work. A watchdog that doesn't bark." Roebuck shook his head. "What a night."

"That's exactly the premise," Stottlemeyer said. "The dog shuts up, it's time to get the gun."

Lovely stuck his head out a window of the police car and demanded to know what was going on.

"Who's that?" Stottlemeyer asked.

"A wino," Finch said.

"I wish," Lovely said.

Roebuck took some money out of his pocket and peeled off two twenties and a ten, and he gave it to Stottlemeyer, who wanted to know what that was for.

"The window."

Stottlemeyer looked at the money. "I'm going to write a letter to somebody about you officers. You're a credit to your uniform. But you don't need to do this. I got insurance."

Roebuck got in behind the wheel. "Forget it. You turn in a claim, the rates go up."

"Thanks again."

"We'll be back with some forms later on," Finch said.

"Let me the hell out of here," Lovely said.

Roebuck started the car and drove away.

Trout found a hose in a toolshed around back and hooked it to a water outlet on the side of the museum.

By placing his thumb over the nozzle, Trout was able to water both trucks with a considerable amount of force.

"It's coming down hard," he said as he sprayed the first truck.

Trout put the nozzle against the crack where the back doors came together on the first truck he watered, hoping to get a few drops inside.

"We better get out of this downpour," he said loudly as he watered the second truck.

"You missed a spot up by the front tire," Annabel said.

After Trout had hosed off both trucks, he turned the water off and rolled the hose up and put it in a flower bed.

He joined Annabel, who was stretched out on her side in the grass, watching.

"It was a long shot," he said. "It didn't work."

"What didn't?"

"Watering the trucks. I thought maybe if they heard the water running, it would make them have to go to the bathroom, and I could hear them scrambling around in there. They *have* been in there awhile now."

"I thought you were washing the trucks," Annabel said, sitting up. "I thought you had gone crazy."

Trout said that *somebody* had to do *something*.

"I'm no good until I get some cigarettes," Annabel said. She was fidgety and had started making strange faces. She'd fill her cheeks full of air and open and close her mouth without speaking. "But I'll tell you one thing. Your earlier ideas were a lot better than these."

"*Damn,*" Trout said.

His face got red. He gritted his teeth and jumped to his feet and pulled a pistol out of his belt and aimed it at the trucks.

And strangely enough, he pulled the trigger.

He shot at the trucks, as Finch had suggested.

At first Annabel thought she was hallucinating.

She turned her head and listened for some type of crash or crack.

Nothing happened.

"You missed," Annabel said, standing up and squinting at the path the bullet had taken, which was evidently *over* the trucks, as there hadn't been even the sound of a bullet tearing into the ground.

Trout was terribly embarrassed at having lost control for a second. He pitched the gun to the ground and sat back down.

"You probably just shot some innocent old lady sleeping in her bed," Annabel said, still squinting at the night.

"The water," an officer by the doors whispered, "is *off*."

"Don't *mention* water," Sergeant House said.

"We need to keep thinking about what they might try next," Lieutenant Bush said. "We need to be prepared. Let your imaginations go."

"What's going to happen," Buck said, "is they'll have to open one of the trucks."

He was in a bad mood from all this sitting around.

Lieutenant Bush said that if they opened the back doors, Pike would be used as a shield.

"Like hell."

"What I'd do," Mounds said, "is back us into a river and drown us and then open the back doors."

"You think we could discuss something besides water for two minutes?" Sergeant House asked.

They decided to play it by ear at the hospital. They decided to go inside and have a look around and then talk things over before they started swiping equipment.

Because of the police uniforms they wore, they assumed they could pretty much have the run of the hospital.

Roebuck found the Emergency sign and pulled the squad car in behind an ambulance. They got out, taking the keys with them so their car wouldn't be stolen. Lovely also got out, dragging his French antique.

"What are you doing?" Finch asked.

"Checking in," Lovely said.

The three of them entered the emergency room area and looked around for signs of life. There was only a nurse sitting at a desk.

"Can I help you?" she asked.

"We're just checking on a couple of things," Finch said, politely removing his hat.

"Nobody has been brought in for an hour," the nurse said. "And the last one was only a lady with gas."

"Somebody held up a store and we thought he might have ducked in here."

"Nobody has run in here."

"Plus," Finch said, grinning, "we could stand a rest room."

The nurse told Finch the rest room was at the end of the hall. The hall was lined with cubicles. These cubicles had curtains for walls. Finch and Roebuck thanked the nurse for her directions and walked down the hall.

Lovely stepped up to the reception desk and said, "I'd like a room, please."

Finch stopped at the first cubicle, pulled the curtains open, and looked inside. There was a fat woman on a table. She was holding her stomach.

"How's it going?" Finch asked.

"I'm dying," the fat woman said.

"You look okay to me."

"Are you a doctor?"

"No, I'm a policeman."

"Then that's why I look okay to you. I'm not committing no crime. That's because I'm dying."

"What's wrong with you?" Roebuck asked.

"It's my stomach. It's blowing up."

"Did they x-ray you?" Finch asked.

"No, that only costs two hundred and fifty dollars. They don't do nothing in this place that doesn't cost five hundred."

"I've got some Tums around here somewhere," Roebuck said, feeling through his pockets.

"Give them all to me."

Roebuck found the Tums and pulled the wrapper from around a couple of tablets. "Here's two," he said, walking to the woman's table.

"Two is for children under five." The fat woman requested, and received, the entire pack and plopped them one by one onto her tongue.

"Well, hang in there," Finch said, motioning for Roebuck to join him back in the hall between the cubicles.

"If you see a machine, get me some more of these things," the fat woman said.

On the way out, Roebuck picked up some gauze and a couple of tubes of ointment from a table, for Trout's head, then he and Finch made their way toward the rest room.

"I hate hospitals," Finch said.

Roebuck agreed. "It's the smell. It reminds me of biology class where we used to slice up frogs."

"I could take the smell without the bodies," Finch said.

Roebuck had to admit the bodies were pretty bad. "It's like walking through a graveyard."

They were tiptoeing.

"It's worse than that," Finch said. "I'm afraid to look around because somebody might drop dead."

"Say," somebody said. The voice came from a cubicle about five yards ahead and to the left.

"Yeah?" Finch walked to the curtain in front of the voice.

"Do you mind?"

"Mind what?"

"Not talking about dead bodies."

"Right," Finch said. "Sorry."

"It's depressing."

"What are you in for?"

"A broken leg."

Finch told the man behind the curtain he had it made. Only one in five million died of that. And since a guy who had one passed away last week, the man in the cubicle had absolutely nothing to worry about.

Roebuck peeked into a cubicle farther up and on the right. He motioned for Finch to join him.

"It's empty," Roebuck whispered.

They were going through some drawers in a cabinet when a doctor wearing a name tag that said Steinberg pushed the curtains open and stepped inside.

"What's going on here?" Steinberg asked.

Finch hopped up on the table and said he had a sprained ankle.

"Where's Buck?" Steinberg asked.

"Sick," Finch said, remembering that Buck was the officer with the baseball cap in the back of one of the trucks.

"That explains why he's not here," Steinberg said, smiling.

"Where?" Roebuck asked.

"Here at the hospital."

"Oh, I get it," Roebuck said. "If you're sick, this is the wrong place to be."

"You catch on quick," Steinberg said, feeling Finch's ankle, which wasn't swollen.

Roebuck wasn't flattered. He was tired of thinking of

excuses and clever answers. He was just about ready to punch somebody in the goddamn nose. And what more appropriate location could he have chosen than a cubicle in an emergency room.

"Did Buck tell you the way it works around here?" Steinberg asked either or both of them. "There's nothing wrong with your ankle, by the way."

"It aches," Finch said.

"The way what works?" Roebuck asked.

"We pay five dollars a body."

Keep it up, Roebuck thought. One more puzzle and somebody is going to get it.

"You pay five dollars a body," Finch repeated.

"Right."

"You must love your work," Roebuck said.

"No, no," Steinberg told him. "You've got it all wrong. We pay you five dollars for every body you take *somewhere else*."

Roebuck looked at Finch.

Finch shook his head slightly. It was a don't-hit-him-yet shake.

"Say there's a gang fight or something like that roughly halfway between here and Mercy Hospital. You guys get the call. You tell the ambulance driver to take the stab wounds to Mercy, you get the five. Five per body, not five apiece."

Steinberg threw back his head and laughed at what was apparently a joke.

Roebuck walked from the cabinet he had been going through to the end of the table where Steinberg stood laughing. Roebuck was a foot taller than the doctor. He reached down and yanked the stethoscope from around the doctor's neck.

"We're on a scavenger hunt," Roebuck said. He walked out of the cubicle, made a left, and headed for the exit.

"My God," Steinberg said, badly shaken. "I thought he was going to hit me."

174

"We don't take bribes," Finch said.

"I've been on call thirteen hours. It was a *joke*."

Finch took a five-dollar bill out of his pocket and tossed it onto the table he had been sitting on. "Actually, he's a hypochondriac," Finch said.

He also headed for the car.

He had to step aside for Lovely, who was being taken somewhere in a wheelchair. Lovely carried the French commode upside down on his lap.

"I just got a shot," Lovely said.

"His blood pressure is very high," the nurse said.

Lovely couldn't *imagine* why. "But I feel tremendous now."

"I feel tremendous too," the fat woman said, opening the curtains to her cubicle. She had her clothes on and was ready to go home.

Roebuck honked from outside.

He had pulled the squad car up to the door.

Finch guessed he had ten seconds before Roebuck would floorboard it.

Finch waved enviously to Lovely as he was wheeled around a corner; and then he walked slowly outside, hoping Roebuck would leave without him.

Trout ran fifty yards to greet the returning squad car.

"You're five minutes early," he said. "How'd it go?"

"Great," Finch said. "How'd it go here?"

"Great," Trout said. "Fantastic."

Roebuck got out and handed Trout the stethoscope.

"What's this?"

"It's a stethoscope," Roebuck said. "You listen to things with it."

"It was all we could get without having our tonsils out," Finch said somberly.

"What the hell am I supposed to do with *this* thing?"

175

"Nothing, we hope," Finch said. "Didn't you figure out which truck was which while we were gone?"

Trout cleared his throat.

"What'd you try?" Roebuck asked.

"A couple of things."

"Like what?" Finch asked.

"Well, I watered the truck."

"You tried to drown them?" Finch asked. "That's worse than trying to shoot them."

"I tried to make them have to go to the bathroom."

"We're in big trouble," Finch said, heading for the museum.

"What about a truck?" Trout asked.

"We didn't see any," Roebuck said, pawing at the ground.

Trout took the stethoscope to one of the trucks. He put the rubber end against a wall and the prongs in his ears. He listened to each truck for about a minute. He walked around the trucks and listened at the other side, and he also crawled underneath the trucks and listened from there.

"What do you hear?" Finch asked.

"The ocean," Trout said. "This thing works like a seashell."

They sat some more on the curb out front.

"Where are my cigarettes?" Annabel asked.

Finch told her they had forgotten, but there was no need to panic. He got up and went to each squad car and returned with their ashtrays.

Annabel searched through the butts, found one that was decent, and puffed away on it.

"We thought of something just before you got back," Trout said. "She did."

Annabel started a second butt from the one she had just finished.

"She found half a cigar over in some bushes and thought of this after the first drag."

"Motion," Annabel said.

"*Motion?*" Finch repeated.

"We bang them around in there," Annabel said.

Trout nodded. "We hit the brakes going ten miles an hour or so. We stand on both sides of the truck and listen. When they start hitting the walls, we hear it, easy."

Roebuck also nodded. "It ought to sound like a popcorn popper in there."

"It's pretty good," Finch said.

Annabel thanked him.

"And I've got a way to make it better." He took the stethoscope from Trout and hooked it around his neck. "We get on top of the truck and listen with the stethoscope. I get some ropes and chains and hook myself to one of the lights on top. That way I can listen while we're moving."

"Ropes and chains," Trout said without enthusiasm. "This is a museum, not a hardware store."

He got a rock out of a flower bed and marked two X's on the driveway. That was where the two people were to stand and listen when he hit the brakes.

"I can't believe it," Finch said. "I'm getting my hopes up again. I thought I was sterile."

"Here they come," Roebuck said.

He and Annabel stood across the driveway from each other, halfway down the hill, on the X's Trout had marked.

"Watch your head," Annabel told him. "Don't get clipped by the side-view mirror."

"I wonder where Finch is?"

"Driving the other truck," Annabel guessed.

Trout kept the speedometer right at ten miles an hour, which was difficult. The truck was in second gear, and it jerked when Trout pressed, or came off, the gas pedal.

He kept both hands on the wheel and saw out of the corner of his eye the kiss Annabel blew.

Roebuck gave him the okay sign.

Trout focused on the stick he had stuck in the ground, and stomped the brakes right on cue. The brakes hissed and the truck skidded a couple of feet at most.

Trout was listening for a loud noise, but he didn't hear anything.

Annabel heard something. She heard one very loud sound, followed by a couple of thuds. "This is the one," she said excitedly.

"You're kidding," Trout said, climbing out of the cab.

"I heard it over here too," Roebuck said from the other side of the truck. "It was loud."

"Now who's so damn smart," Annabel said, slapping the side of the van a few times with her palm. "How's it going in there now?"

"Did *you* hear it?" Trout asked, looking up.

Roebuck walked around the front of the truck and said again that yeah, he heard it loud and clear.

"Not you. Hey, Finch, did you hear them in there?" Trout continued to look up at the top of the truck.

"He's not up there," Annabel said.

"Yeah, he is. I helped tie him on with the garden hose. Hey, Finch."

"Nobody is up there," Roebuck said. "We could see the top of the truck all the way down the hill."

It didn't take them long to discover what had made the noises when Trout hit the brakes. It was Finch's head banging against the back doors. Finch had positioned himself on his stomach near the middle of the rig with the hose tight around an ankle so that when Trout stopped, he would not shoot forward and perhaps be run over. The hose had been tied to a taillight at the back of the truck. But the top was slick from the drizzle, and when Trout shifted from first gear into second, Finch slid over the side and then on around behind, where he now dangled upside down, a few yards above the ground. The back of Finch's head had smashed the doors once, hard, but after that Finch was able to brace himself and absorb many of the additional blows with his arms, which about broke both wrists. When he had first slid over the back, he'd started to call out for help, but he hadn't wanted to jeopardize the whole project.

So they found him hanging there, his face purple, his arms limp.

"Cut the son of a bitch down," Trout said.

Roebuck carried Finch to a soft spot in the grass. Finch said that he was okay, except for a little blurred vision. "Did anybody hear anything inside?"

"We heard your head hitting the doors," Roebuck said.

Since there was always the possibility that the police were in the *other* truck, Trout returned the first vehicle to the gravel lot beside the museum and tried the second one.

Annabel and Roebuck again took positions on either side of the driveway.

Trout again hit the brakes at the stick.

Annabel and Roebuck leaned toward the skidding truck and listened intently.

Trout got out and checked with them.

"Nothing," Annabel said.

"Same here," Roebuck said. "Zilch."

Lieutenant Bush shielded the glow from the lighter with his left hand and moved softly through the bodies, congratulating his people.

They were all flat on their stomachs, each one holding on to the arms or legs of the person next to him.

Or her.

They were wedged tightly together on the floor like pieces of a jigsaw puzzle.

When the truck had stopped suddenly, nobody had slid.

179

Somebody had giggled, though.

Lieutenant Bush stopped next to Pike, who was stretched flat along with everyone else. "Nice work," he said.

Pike nodded.

"How could you have known they'd hit the brakes and listen for us to tumble around?"

"Hell," Buck whispered, "he's one of them."

"Yeah, but that was before I was deputized," Pike said. "Before I was pardoned."

Grosvenor studied his audience and glanced out the corner of his eye at his wife and assistant, who were off to the left on the sidewalk.

Charlotte smiled and nodded.

Grosvenor buttoned his suit coat and stepped to the microphone.

Several reporters stood by their cameramen.

"The night shift . . ." Grosvenor said dramatically.

Charlotte held up her hand.

Grosvenor stopped talking.

A late-arriving TV news crew pulled up to the curb. Grosvenor waited while their microphone was set up.

"The night shift at the Thirty-third Precinct has been *kidnapped*."

One of the reporters said, "Brother."

Another reporter said, "Oh, no."

One of the cameramen moved in tighter.

"From what we have been able to put together at this point," Grosvenor continued, "approximately fifteen heavily armed terrorists attacked this building several hours ago."

Grosvenor paused and looked at the shattered glass door that he himself had bashed in.

"All our people are alive, and they are being held for six million dollars in ransom."

"What do you think?" Charlotte asked Rick quietly.

He had been downstairs comforting the Charles Emerson party and coordinating the arrival of officers from adjoining precincts. He had missed quite a lot.

"It's perfect," Rick said. "They'd never believe we could have made this thing up. I don't know how you ever thought of it."

"Practice," Charlotte said, smiling at her husband. "We've been married twelve years."

"And it even gets us off the hook with the lawsuit. Cops didn't lock those people downstairs. Maniacs did."

Charlotte nodded and continued smiling.

"It takes care of everything except the strike."

"We're going to settle that out of our own pocket. It won't amount to all that much."

"Maybe we should tell those people who are striking what's going on," Rick said.

"We will when they call in," Charlotte told him.

"What about me?" Moon asked.

"An extra week's vacation."

"I'll take it," Moon said.

Charlotte nodded.

They quit whispering.

Grosvenor was saying, firmly and with perfect posture:

"This city will *not* be blackmailed."

"You mean to say you're going to refuse even to negotiate for the lives of your officers?" a reporter asked.

"If we paid these terrorists millions of dollars in ransom, the thousands of other people who are employed by this city would become fair game from that moment on."

"You're saying somebody just walked in and took an entire *precinct?*" another reporter asked.

"It would be no more difficult than kidnapping a building full of reporters," Grosvenor answered.

"Yeah, but you people have *guns.*"

Grosvenor frowned. "We're not allowed to draw them

until we have reasonable cause. Like a wound. We're fortunate to be able to carry bullets these days. Besides, kidnappers don't wear name tags. The police were outnumbered."

"If this doesn't get us elected, nothing will," Rick said.

Trout opened and shuffled the deck of playing cards he had found in a desk drawer in the security room.

Finch leaned forward and stared at the cards, as though Trout might try to cheat.

"This isn't fair," Annabel said. "I don't know how to drive one of those big damn things."

Finch, still squinting at the cards as Trout cut them, said, "It's simple, I'll teach you."

Trout shuffled some more.

Finch wanted to know if aces where high or low.

"High," Trout answered, spreading the cards face down on the desk. "High card picks a truck and takes it somewhere and looks in the back. Ladies first."

Annabel started to draw a card but stopped to wipe her palms on her shirt. She looked at the cards for a couple of seconds and pulled one toward her.

"*Ace!*" Finch said as Annabel turned the card over.

The card was a trey.

Finch shook his head.

Annabel gave him a dirty look.

Roebuck went next. He didn't mess around. He yanked a card from the middle of the pile and flipped it.

It was the jack of clubs.

"*That's* more like it," Finch said.

Trout had a sip of water and drew the card closest to him. He turned one edge of the card up and peeked at it as though he were a riverboat gambler.

He smiled and said, "It's a four."

Finch stood up and leaned across the table and turned Trout's card. It was a king, the king of hearts.

Finch smiled.

Trout tried to slip the king back into the pile.

Finch took the king of hearts and wadded it up and tossed it into a garbage can.

"Next," Annabel said.

"I should have diplomatic immunity," Trout said.

Finch told him he had it all wrong. Since all of this had been his idea, he should *have* to go.

"Next," Annabel said again.

Her eyes were closed.

"What are you doing?" Finch asked.

"She's putting a hex on you, I think," Roebuck said.

Annabel said nothing. She rocked slowly from side to side in her chair.

"Hex my butt," Finch said.

He ran his fingers over the pile of cards several times as if he were trying to feel through them. He pulled two cards toward him and felt the back of each one. "One is a deuce. I'd stake my life on it."

"Come on, flip it," Trout said.

Finch touched the cards gently one more time and turned over the one to his right.

Roebuck laughed.

Trout fanned himself.

"It worked," Roebuck said to Annabel.

She opened her eyes and looked at the ace of diamonds that was in front of Finch, whose face was buried in his hands.

Annabel reached across the table and flipped the card Finch had almost chosen.

It was the ace of spades.

"You think we ought to tell him about the other one?" Roebuck said.

"There's no need to punish him." Trout put the ace of spades back into the pile.

"I wonder what the odds are on getting *two* of them?" Roebuck asked.

"Astronomical," Annabel said.

Finch sat behind the wheel of the truck nearest the museum, frowning. He had taken off his policeman's shirt and was wearing a windbreaker zipped up to his neck.

"Now what you do," Trout told him, "is drive a few miles away. Open the truck and have a look and then get the hell out of there."

"Give me some damn money," Finch said, "so maybe I can find somebody and pay them to open the doors. Maybe that way I won't get shot at close range. If I can be running in the same direction as the bullet, maybe it won't go all the way through me."

"That's a *fine* idea," Trout said. "See, these things happen for a reason. Nobody else would have thought of looking for somebody to pay."

Trout collected some cash and handed it to Finch.

"Now listen, if this truck is empty, bring it back fast and we'll start loading. But if the police are in the back, well, Finch, you're pretty much on your own. What you ought to do is call us and get a cab back as soon as you can."

Finch looked at Trout with a very bitter expression. "I can't call. I ripped out the phone wires, remember?"

"Oops," Trout said.

Finch's eyes widened. "I'm out there fighting for my life and all you can say is for Christ's sake *oops?*"

"Let's play it this way," Annabel suggested, starting another of the butts she carried in a sack. "If he's not back in half an hour, we'll assume the police were in his truck and that he was injured or killed."

Trout said, "Or on the run."

Annabel asked Roebuck what he thought.

"It sounds all right to me."

184

Finch wanted to know what all this chitchat was, a PTA meeting?

He started the truck he was in, and moved it ten or fifteen yards. He got out, slammed the door, and asked Trout to change keys with him. "I'm taking the other truck."

"Fine," Trout said. "Good luck."

Finch climbed into the other van, slammed the door shut, and drove toward the gate—too fast, Annabel thought.

They watched the taillights disappear.

"Isn't your first guess on a true-or-false test usually the right one?" Roebuck asked.

Six

Trout looked at the keys Finch had exchanged just seconds ago and said, "My God."

He turned and ran.

He ran from the hallway to the squad car parked by the statue out front. He jumped into the car and skidded across the lawn before heading for the gate.

He couldn't believe he hadn't told Finch to take the truck to a specific place in case something like this happened, but a person couldn't think of everything.

Finch was gone by the time Trout got to the gate. The gate was almost gone. Finch had blasted through it at a considerable rate of speed. Trout pulled both sections of the wrought-iron gate together and tied them in place with his shirt. Then he drove back up the hill full throttle, passing Annabel and Roebuck about half a block from the museum.

They were carrying paintings.

They were going home.

Annabel had six or seven small ones, and Roebuck was dragging a few large pieces of art behind him in a blanket.

"I think he's naked," Roebuck said as Trout sped by.

Trout cut left in front of the fountain and skidded on around to the side of the museum where the van was parked. He stomped the brakes and got out, wondering if one small bit of luck every twenty or thirty years was too much to ask for.

He climbed onto the truck's back bumper, grabbed the handle, closed his eyes, and yanked.

The handle turned.

Trout swung the door open and looked inside, not that it was necessary.

"You don't lock an empty truck," Trout said, wrapping a padded blanket around a small painting.

Quackenbush and Mickey had been brought from the closet to help with the loading. They were blinking at the bright lights.

Trout had moved the truck to the front door.

It was empty.

Annabel and Roebuck stood just inside the museum and looked from the empty truck to Trout. They'd been planning to drive the police car home—until Trout came around the corner in the van.

"You lock a truck with something important in the back," he said. "Something important like the police."

Trout picked up a bust and handed it to Quackenbush so it could be properly wrapped and tied.

"Go slow," Roebuck said.

Trout stretched. "When we put the police in the back of one of the trucks at the precinct, we locked the back doors." He pretended to turn a key.

"Naturally," Roebuck said.

"Out there in the parking lot a second ago, I climbed on

187

the bumper and pulled the handle down. It moved, which meant there was nothing inside the truck."

Roebuck frowned and said, "Now, if the truck had been locked. . . ."

"Then I couldn't have turned the handle. If I couldn't have turned the handle, that would have meant the police were inside. We never locked the empty truck. There was no reason. It's human nature."

"You don't lock an empty truck," Roebuck said.

"No," Trout said.

"We thought you cracked up. We thought you were opening the back doors for the hell of it and were going to shoot it out with them if they were in there."

"I'm out of bullets, remember?"

Roebuck nodded.

"You might have said something," Annabel said.

Trout told her that although he had figured out how to tell which truck was which, the one outside still could have contained the police, and he didn't want to get everybody excited before there was a reason.

"You ought to be very proud of yourself," Roebuck said.

"Better late than never, I guess," Trout said quietly.

Annabel looked at what still had to be wrapped and said, "Yeah, it's too bad about Finch. Somebody help me with this Chagall."

Finch spotted a cab, couldn't believe it, but nevertheless pulled his truck in behind.

The cab driver was reading a magazine.

"Are you on duty?" Finch asked.

"Sure," the kid said, tossing his magazine aside. "Where to?"

"This is a little hard to explain. Nowhere."

"Nowhere? I don't understand."

188

Finch handed the driver a ten-dollar bill. "I'm paying you to sit here."

"Why?"

"Because I don't want a ride now."

"Oh."

"But I might want a ride later."

"Now I understand."

"Sit here ten minutes. If I haven't come back, keep the ten and you're on your own. If I want a ride, I'll be back before then."

The cab driver looked at the truck and nodded.

"What if you come back in fifteen minutes and I'm still here?"

"You don't get an extra five, that's for damn sure."

"Then after ten minutes, I'll leave, whether I have a fare or not."

"It's your gas," Finch said, returning to his truck.

"Don't get sore," the cab driver said.

Finch told the kid he'd find him and run him over if he left this spot a second before the ten minutes was up.

Three blocks from the cab, Finch found a candidate for opening the doors. A man was sitting by an intersection, under an awning, folding newspapers. The awning was in front of a coffee shop. Somebody was inside the coffee shop getting ready to open for business.

God, Finch thought, the sun was actually bearing down on them!

He pulled the truck to the right-hand curb and rolled down the passenger window.

"How would you like to make," Finch said, counting his money, "more than a hundred dollars?"

"First," the man said without looking up, "I throw papers. In the rain. In the snow. In anything. Then I go from the gutter here to a place called Tidewater Finance where I work from ten until five. I call people and tell them they're overdue with their payments. Do you know how much money some of our customers borrow?"

"No," Finch said.

"Twenty dollars, thirty dollars. Can you believe that amount of money can mean so *much* to a person?"

"Yes," Finch said. "Listen, pal. Give me a break."

"After that, I go home and sell things like light bulbs over the phone. Light bulbs and dimmer switches and extension cords. Do you know that last night I called somebody and tried to sell them some light bulbs and told them I was *crippled?*"

"How could I know that," Finch said.

"I've got four children," the man folding newspapers said.

Finch asked the man again if he'd like to make some money.

"Yeah, how long would it take?"

"Fifteen minutes."

"I haven't got time."

"Give me a damn paper," Finch said.

The man tossed a newspaper inside the truck and Finch tossed him a five-dollar bill and drove off.

"You need any light bulbs?" the man asked.

Finch drove back by the taxi and handed the driver another ten.

"Thank you, sir," the driver said.

If something didn't develop soon, Finch was going to run out of money.

"Follow me this time," he said to the cab driver.

"Okay."

"If I stop, you stop."

"And in ten more minutes you give me ten more dollars."

"Eight dollars," Finch said.

"Ten."

"I don't see anybody else looking for a cab."

"There are no other cabs."

Finch agreed on the ten dollars.

Finch drove two blocks, made a right, and spotted a bakery truck waiting for a light. He stepped on it and thought about ramming the bakery truck but pulled alongside it instead and waved the driver over.

The bakery truck pulled to the curb.

Finch pulled in front of him.

The cab pulled up and the driver asked what he was supposed to do now.

Finch told the cab driver to go straight for a block and a half and pull around the second corner up there and wait.

"You've only got six minutes left on the second ten."

Finch gave the driver five dollars more and joined the baker on the sidewalk. The baker, whose name was Abe Ginsberg, was wiping moisture off his glasses.

"What can I do for you?" he asked. "I don't sell any singles out of the truck. All I have unaccounted for this morning is five dozen glazed."

Finch got right to the point. He counted his money again and said, "How would you like to make a hundred and fifty dollars?"

Abe Ginsberg replaced his glasses and said to himself, "At five o'clock in the morning I'm the one who meets a psycho who thinks he's a game show host."

"I'm no game show host," Finch said, smiling slightly. "And I'm serious about the hundred and a half."

"That's a hundred and fifty *dollars*, not a hundred dollars and fifty *cents*."

"Right."

Abe Ginsberg said that was a lot of doughnuts. It was three hundred and seventy-five doughnuts retailing at forty cents apiece.

"Open the back of this truck and the one fifty is yours." Finch held out the money, which was mostly twenties.

Abe Ginsberg raised his eyebrows and looked at it. He looked from the money to the truck. "Whose truck is it?"

"It's rented," Finch said.

"What's in the truck?"

Finch didn't have time to dream up anything elaborate— the time or the ability. "There might be police in it."

Abe Ginsberg looked at his watch.

"But it doesn't matter if they *are* in there. They won't do anything to you."

"They might take the hundred and fifty."

"They won't even know you have it," Finch said.

Abe Ginsberg studied the money some more. "Is this illegal?"

"How could letting some police out be illegal?"

"Interesting point," Abe Ginsberg said, taking the money from Finch. He stacked the bills according to their worth, with the twenties on top. "You said there *might* be some police in the truck."

Finch shrugged.

"So that means there might *not*."

"Right. You get the one fifty either way. That's not bad money for opening an empty truck."

"I got a couple of more questions here."

"The other part of the deal," Finch said, "is no more questions. You put the key in the lock and turn it left and yank the handle down. Give me a couple of minutes before you open the back door."

The baker looked at the truck again.

"Come on," Finch said. "There are plenty of people out there who need the one fifty."

"You'd have to wake them up."

Abe Ginsberg folded the money.

Finch said he had ten seconds to make a decision.

"So this might almost be my civic duty, letting some police out."

"That's exactly right. You'll get a plaque. You'll be on television."

Abe Ginsberg stuffed the money into his pocket and turned his back on Finch.

Finch ran.

He ran as hard as he could for roughly twenty yards.

He stopped.

He trotted back to where the baker stood with his back turned.

"I need ten dollars of my money back," Finch said.

"That hurts."

Abe Ginsberg handed the ten spot backwards over his shoulder.

Finch took off running again.

He was in soft shape and ran as hard as he could for forty yards, then weaved the rest of the way to where the cab was parked. He got in the backseat and looked at the truck.

"Back up four feet," he wheezed.

The driver positioned the cab so that Finch could see through the rear window what was going on back there, without being observed.

"Perfect," Finch said.

"What is it we're doing now?" the cab driver asked.

"I'm looking out the window. You're making ten more dollars."

Finch handed the driver the last ten.

"This is my first time driving a cab, sir," the driver said. "You're even my first fare. Sorry for all the questions. I've got a degree in public relations, but I got laid off last week."

"You really screwed up, didn't you?" Finch said. "What you should have taken in school was driver's ed."

"You're not up to anything weird are you?" the driver asked.

"Don't worry, kid, this kind of thing happens all the time," Finch told him.

Abe Ginsberg waited until he could no longer hear Finch's footsteps.

He went to the back of the truck and leaned toward the doors and said:

"This guy driving the truck stops me and says he wants me to open these doors here. He says there might be police inside. This is all I know. I'm a baker. I've got some nice fresh chocolate longjohns with me. Don't shoot, come out and have some pastries. They're the best in the world. What do you think about that?"

Abe Ginsberg put an ear to the door and listened.

"Is anybody home?"

He put the hundred and forty dollars in his left shoe and climbed onto the back bumper. He put the key in the lock.

"The only thing I want for this is a squad car to come by my place about closing time once in a while, is that okay? Just cruise by, make sure nobody's robbing me. That's when it happens, at closing time. A squad car driving by, and maybe some kind of plaque for the window—a plaque or a picture of somebody important in the department. I got a shot of Don Ho in my front window. You ever hear of him? He's this singer. He comes in two years ago looking for directions and my wife takes a snapshot of him with his arm around me, eating a roll. You know what? The week after we got the picture up, we sell pineapple turnovers by the wheelbarrowful. Any of you guys in there ever hear of Don Ho?"

Abe Ginsberg turned the key.

"Let me tell you one thing. This guy's teeth are better than his voice. He eats seven doughnuts and then sings a couple of bars of a bubble song. Ten million dogs start howling."

Abe Ginsberg hopped to the ground.

Both back doors flew open simultaneously.

Two men stood flattened against the sidewalls by the back door. Another man was lying on his stomach, pointing a gun. The gun was pointed at Abe Ginsberg. Yet another man near the doors was wearing underwear.

"Don't anybody move," Lieutenant Bush said, stepping forward.

"It's only me," Abe Ginsberg said. "The baker."

"I said stand still."

"I got an extra smock in the van," Abe Ginsberg said to the man wearing boxer shorts.

"Go," Finch said as the police began piling out of the truck. He hadn't remembered there were that many of them. He hadn't remembered they were that big. They certainly hadn't been as angry the last time Finch saw them.

The cab driver wanted to know what was going on back there.

"God, it looks like they're storming a beach," Finch muttered to himself.

"*What?*" the cab driver said.

Finch told him to go, and he kicked the back of the driver's seat.

They went.

The police grilled Abe Ginsberg until he became too tough and folded his arms and demanded to see a lawyer, of which, incidentally, there were four in his family.

They grilled him on the sidewalk.

195

"My doughnuts are getting cold," he said.

"So are mine," Mounds said. The smock from the bakery truck came only to his knees.

"Tell us again," Lieutenant Bush said, taking notes on a pad from the bakery truck.

"The guy in this truck stops me. He waves and pulls me over. We get out. I try to sell him five dozen glazed doughnuts. He say there might be police in the back. He gives me a key. He runs. I unlock the doors. You start driving me crazy. That's where we are now."

Lieutenant Bush told Abe Ginsberg to wait there. He led his people along the sidewalk a ways.

"We might be all right," Lieutenant Bush said solemnly. "But on the other hand, we might not."

Buck straightened the bill on his ball cap. He looked around. "We'll be all right when we get the sons of bitches who stole us."

"Who *what?*" Abe Ginsberg asked.

Lieutenant Bush moved his people farther down the block. "We're okay if they haven't done a crime."

"You only get a *ticket* for kidnapping?" Pike asked.

"*Another* crime. Let's hear what you people think. Quietly."

Everybody thought for a few seconds.

"Maybe they gave up and went home," Heather said.

Lieutenant Bush found that premise unlikely. If they were going home, they wouldn't have unlocked the doors.

"Maybe they're stealing something that was stolen in the first place," Billows guessed. "Something that would never be reported."

"What they're doing is wiping out a bank while we stand here playing twenty questions," Buck said.

Sergeant House told Buck to get a grip on himself before somebody else did. "The worst thing that could possibly happen would be for us to catch them now. We'd have to explain the way they walked in and made fools of us."

Mounds rubbed his hands and knees together, looked at his watch, and said that the next shift wouldn't begin drifting in for a good half hour.

"Here's what we do," Sergeant House said. "We go back. We check the computers. If nothing's there, if no crime has been committed by these people, the lieutenant leads us in a prayer and we go off duty."

Buck thought that was contemptible.

"Listen, Buck," Sergeant House said. "You get to write the minority opinion. Write it in your diary. Go chase them on your vacation."

Lieutenant Bush stepped between his officers before there was a fistfight.

He ordered everybody into the bakery truck. This order was easier conceived than executed. Pastries were all over the place, and there were no seats in the back of the panel truck.

"The reason House wants to go back to the precinct is so he can ride with the apple turnovers," Billows said.

The bigger people sat down first. The smaller people sat on the bigger ones' laps. Lieutenant Bush was the last to squeeze his way inside. He handed boxes of doughnuts and things to the smaller people sitting on laps, so he could clear a path to the front of the truck, where he said:

"All right, let's go."

"I don't turn the key without guaranteed mileage," Abe Ginsberg said.

Finch told the cab driver, whose name was Tony, to stop and let him out a block from the museum. Finch didn't want to act suspicious.

Nothing is easy, Finch decided as he got out of the cab. Everything is torture.

Tony let Finch out, thanked him for his business, put the cab in park, and started reading a magazine.

Finch stared at the cab for a couple of seconds. He had planned to run, but with the cab sitting there like that he couldn't.

So Finch knocked on the passenger window.

"Where to?" Tony asked.

"Kennedy," Finch said.

"This has been an unbelievable morning. Hop in."

"Not me, you," Finch said.

Once the taxi was out of sight—Finch had told Tony about the planeloads of foreigners that would be arriving at this time of the morning, and about how he could drive them in through New Jersey without their even knowing it and collect big money—Finch ran.

He hated running too.

The last time he had run for an extended period of time was in junior high when he had tried out for the basketball team. He had run two laps around the basketball court and quit. Running was bad for your insides. It was bad for your feet. It was bad for your mind. Finch guessed that people ran so that when they got to be eighty-eight, they could stay alive three more days because they had been in perfect condition back when they were thirty-nine. Running was like having facelift after facelift. It was depressing. It also hurt.

By the time Finch got to the front gates of the museum, his right side was stinging and he was winded. He squeezed through the gates Trout had tied together with a shirt and leaned against them and rubbed his left calf, which had tightened up.

He then took on the hill.

A quarter of the way up he lost his right shoe. He retrieved it and almost started tumbling back down the hill to the gate. Although the incline was slight at this point, perhaps five degrees, Finch didn't have much balance left and he had to fight to regain his momentum, insignificant as it was.

Halfway up the hill he twisted his ankle. At that point it felt as though somebody were hitting the bottoms of his feet with golf clubs, so he swung right and ran on the grass instead of the pavement. He stepped on a rock, nearly fell, but kept going.

Three-quarters of the way up Finch swore violently as he wondered why he hadn't used the damn intercom next to the gate to call up the news that his truck had the police in it. Had he done that, he could have *walked* up. Hell, they would have come down and *driven* him up.

By the time he could see the front door, his vision was terrible. He was weaving. He felt as if he were falling from a great height. Everything was swirling.

"My truck," he tried to shout. "My truck. My truck."

As Finch reached flat ground he brought his knees up as high as he could, and churned his arms and ran chin up for the blur of light from the museum's front doorway.

So this is what running is all about, Finch thought as the light from the door began hopping up and down and then sideways. This is what Olympians feel as they cross the finish line with thousands of people cheering.

It *was* exhilarating.

Finch felt a tremendous sense of accomplishment as he ran into Trout's arms and was dragged the last few yards to the front steps. "They're out," Finch whispered. "They were in my truck."

"You did a tremendous job," Trout said. "I'm very proud of you."

Finch could speak only two words at a time. He told Trout that he had paid a baker to open the back doors. He tried to describe the sight of the police officers leaping onto the sidewalk but became confused and shut up.

Trout supported Finch and guided him to the front steps.

Finch leaned against the building and closed his eyes. He was flushed and breathing in gulps.

"Hey, Finch is back," Trout said.

"No kidding," Roebuck said. He was inside the front hallway. "That's great."

"The more the merrier," Annabel said. She was inside the truck, loading something. The truck was backed against the steps. She walked to the doors and stuck her head outside and said, "You want to give us a hand?"

Finch opened his eyes and looked at Annabel, who was hanging out the back of the truck.

Roebuck stuck his head out the front door. "The police are out?"

Finch squinted, rubbed his eyes, and squinted again. He nodded. He nodded about half an inch.

Roebuck smiled. "Then I guess that means the strike is over."

Trout smiled too. "Yeah. But we still need to hurry. They'll probably get things figured out before *too* long."

"Yeah, you're probably right," Roebuck agreed. "A couple or three days, they'll put their finger right on it."

Finch looked from Annabel to Roebuck to Trout to the truck. He held his hand out. Trout took it and helped Finch to his feet. Finch brushed Trout away and walked painfully to the back of the truck, holding his left side and his right thigh.

He stopped and looked up and down at the truck. He touched one of the doors, which was wide open. He leaned right and looked inside the truck. About a dozen pieces of art had been loaded, including the bust of Alexander the Great. Finch picked it up and looked at it. He put it down and turned to Trout and said:

"What's this goddamn thing doing open?"

❖ ❖ ❖

Abe Ginsberg pulled sharply to the curb, jammed his truck into park, and asked for a mileage voucher.

There was no passenger seat in the truck, so Lieutenant Bush had to step over a box of sugar doughnuts and lean forward to see what was going on at his precinct.

"God Almighty," he said. "Go." He saw the chief of police standing just inside the front door. He saw three or four cars and vans belonging to television stations. He saw microphones.

"I'm not going anywhere," Abe Ginsberg said, stomping the emergency brake. He also took the keys out of the ignition.

"It's the chief," Lieutenant Bush said. "*It's everybody.*"

Buck told them they should have gone after the bastards.

Abe Ginsberg got out of the bakery truck.

Lieutenant Bush grabbed at him and missed.

"Somebody *do* something," Sergeant House said.

Lieutenant Bush ducked out of sight. The only thing he could think to do was to look as pitiful as possible. Buck's head was still red from where he had fallen on Pike, so Lieutenant Bush positioned the slightly injured officer near the front door.

"Now just remember," Lieutenant Bush said. "We haven't done anything."

"We got stolen and came back in a doughnut truck," Sergeant House said.

Abe Ginsberg walked right up to the chief, whom he recognized from television, and stuck out his hand.

Rick shook the baker's hand because the chief was busy thinking about his next statement to the reporters, and asked, "What do you want?"

"This is more like it," Abe Ginsberg said pleasantly. "It's the first question I've heard in a long time. Before, all I got was orders. Do this. Drive there. I appreciate the courteous question."

"Get that truck out of here," Grosvenor said.

"Here we go again."

"It's in a no-parking zone," Rick said. "Nobody ordered any doughnuts."

"Dozens of people ordered doughnuts. They're probably wondering where they are."

"What do you want?" Grosvenor asked. He was still glowing because of the way he had handled his kidnapping announcement.

"A picture, I think," Abe Ginsberg said. "I got two now, one of Don Ho and one of Wayne Newton. Do you know what this Newton writes on my picture the last time we were in Las Vegas? He writes 'Best Wishes, Ace.' My name is Abe. Newton, he is some kind of businessman, though. You know why everybody goes and sees his shows? I'll tell you why. Once a year he throws a tremendous party for all the cab drivers in town. They stay all night and drink free whiskey and eat free food, so what are you going to say when somebody gets in your cab and asks what show is good? You're going to say Newton is the best there is. Maybe what I should do is get the telephone operators into my place and let them eat a couple of hundred dollars' worth of cinnamon rolls. Maybe then when somebody calls in for the number of a bakery, the operators will say forget Carpellas, those people use holes the size of hockey pucks, go see old Abe, he's the best there is. What do you think about that?"

"Impound the truck," Grosvenor said.

"You better go," Rick said. "We're busy."

Abe Ginsberg folded his arms. "I'm not going anywhere until you get those people out of my truck."

"People," Rick said, squinting at the truck. "What people?"

"*Your* people. There's some in uniforms. There's a woman. There's one in underpants. *That's* who's in my truck. They're eating their way through it like ants."

Grosvenor blinked.

Once.

Rick told him to stay where he was, and he ran down the

steps. He stuck his head in the driver's window. The people in the bakery truck shied away from him.

"Who are you?" Rick asked.

"What do you mean who are we?" Sergeant House asked back. "Who are *you?*"

"The chief's assistant."

"We're the police," Lieutenant Bush said.

"This man is injured and needs medical attention," Sergeant House said, pointing at Buck's head.

Rick stood up and looked around. He leaned back down and told them not to move. He told them that if anybody strolled by casually and asked them who they were and what they were doing, they were to roll the windows up and lock the doors.

"What's all the excitement?" Mounds asked conversationally.

"I thought your sorry excuses were going to call back."

Nobody said anything.

Rick turned and ran back up the steps.

"There were no phones in the back of the truck, you flunkie," Sergeant House said after Rick was out of range.

"It's them," Rick told the chief.

"Move them," Charlotte said. "Get them out of here, *fast.* You know what to say, Clark. *Hurry.*"

"I wonder why they didn't call," Grosvenor said.

"Let's go," Rick said to Abe Ginsberg, who said he wasn't going anywhere without having his picture taken.

Abe Ginsberg drove here and there. He weaved around and drove generally away from the Thirty-third Precinct.

Grosvenor said without looking back:

"You know what I thought walking down the steps? That you people were part of a conspiracy, that you were hired to pull this by somebody who is going to run against me in the primary."

He turned around suddenly and four or five officers jumped back.

"Here's the way we're going to handle this strike of yours. I'll pay you personally one hundred and thirty dollars a month. There is no negotiating. I'll pay Bush the first of every month. Which one of you is Bush?"

Lieutenant Bush tried to smile.

"This is gutless, Bush."

Lieutenant Bush quit smiling and looked at Sergeant House whose eyebrows were raised.

As were Heather's.

"Regarding homosexuals, you're going to have to get by with what you have. Your demand for a homosexual is denied."

Lieutenant Bush glanced to his left and right and saw people shrugging. They only shrugged a little, but Lieutenant Bush shrugged back.

"Your request to have the bathroom painted is taken under consideration."

Nobody understood, or said, a word.

"The people who had their purses snatched threatened to sue us for many millions, but we fixed that too. We fixed it very nicely. *You* didn't lock those people up. The kidnappers did."

Everybody but Pike frowned.

"You're probably wondering *what* kidnappers."

Even Pike frowned at that.

"We made up a kidnapping. Roughly fifteen heavily armed people took you to a warehouse and demanded a ransom of six million dollars. Do you have that?"

Nobody said a word.

"Do you *have* that?"

Lieutenant Bush managed a nod and barely kept from falling over forward.

"We refused to be blackmailed. The kidnappers got frustrated. You escaped. Make it good. You jumped into the East River and swam six blocks. We'll take you somewhere now. Wait a half hour and come in. Are there any questions?"

Pike was the only one who moved, and it was fifteen or twenty seconds before he did. He held up his hand.

"About this one thirty a month," Pike said. "Are we talking about cash here or what?"

"What's your name?" Grosvenor asked.

"My name is Pike."

"How long have you been with the department?"

"Not long."

"If you don't keep quiet about the money, you won't be around long enough to get any."

"For the love of God, don't fire me," Pike said.

Sergeant House cleared his throat and said he lived around the corner to the right two blocks.

Abe Ginsberg made a right and pulled up in front of House's building.

Nobody knew quite what to do then, so they sat quietly until Grosvenor told them to get the hell off the street for the next half hour or so.

They got out.

"The key to this," Grosvenor said, "is that the phony kidnappers lost all hope when I refused to pay the ransom. Make your escape dramatic but within reason."

They stood in a line on the sidewalk and watched the chief of police give them a look of total disgust; and they watched as the bakery truck drove away and made a left at the first corner.

Then they watched a couple of other things—a building or two and a stoplight and a parked car.

They had a hunch they were heroes.

✿　✿　✿

"How would you like a color picture for your front window?" Grosvenor asked Abe Ginsberg as they headed back to the Thirty-third Precinct.

"Of you eating a ninety-five-cent cherry twist? I'd love it."

Finch, Roebuck, and Annabel carried artwork from the front hallway to the back of the truck and handed it to Quackenbush's assistant, Mickey, who in turn passed the masterpieces on to Trout and Quackenbush, who were inside the van.

Quackenbush was methodical with his wrapping. Once he had a padded blanket around a piece of art, he used tape to further secure the corners.

Trout was much more casual, and Quackenbush had to rewrap a large oil painting to cover its back completely.

"You do know that if somebody puts so much as a nick on anything, it's going to reduce its value a great deal," Quackenbush said, taping a blanket around a Matisse.

"That's one of the things I wanted to talk to you about," Trout said. "If we see any kind of police between now and when we get where we're going, I'll climb back here and start slashing."

The prospect of that made Quackenbush slightly ill. He closed his eyes and composed himself and nodded. He asked Trout to be sure and close the front doors at the museum so no one else could wander in and take what was left.

"All you do is pull them to," Quackenbush said.

Trout said that he remembered exactly how the front doors closed and locked. "After the next shift comes on, you'll need to be sure and hook the telephone wires back together. We'll call before noon. We're going to want about thirty percent of this stuff's net worth transferred to an account overseas."

Quackenbush nodded and taped another blanket around a painting.

"We've got a problem," Annabel said. She put a vase on a blanket. Her expression was not pleasant.

Trout left Quackenbush to his wrapping and climbed out of the truck. Before he asked Annabel what the problem was, he looked at what had been loaded and at his watch.

"How much is in?"

"About two-thirds of what we planned originally." Annabel folded her master list and tucked it into her back pocket.

"That ought to do it," Trout said.

Annabel nodded. "I agree. That's the problem."

She led Trout back into the front hallway, where Finch was pushing, or, more accurately, *attempting* to push, a gigantic rug that was mounted on some heavy boards. This arrangement was about nine feet tall and almost as wide. Finch shoved as hard as he could, and moved the rug and boards several inches.

He peeked around a board and said, "I found this by the kitchen. It was some English king's."

"He's gone out of his head with greed," Annabel said.

Trout told Finch, firmly, to put it back.

"There's no way. I got a favor or two coming. When you people figured out which truck was empty, you could have honked."

"You were gone," Trout said.

"I about got trampled to death out there. What's ten more minutes, anyway?"

Finch pushed the rug and boards another inch toward the door.

"It's too big and it's too late," Trout said.

Finch kept shoving the rug. "After I get this in the truck, I'm going back downstairs. There's a room down there full of more great small stuff. There's some kind of ruins and bones worth a fortune that I can stick in my pockets."

Trout called Roebuck back from the truck and told him

to start locking the guards back in the closet. "Lock them in different closets."

"Right," Roebuck said.

He went outside and returned with Mickey. Roebuck led him into the security room, which had two closets.

"Start turning the lights off," Trout told Annabel.

She nodded and wandered off.

Finch tried to hurry with his rug, but it tilted left and fell flat against the floor. Finch had to jump out of the way. He got down on his hands and knees and tried to shove the rug along that way.

"We're leaving," Trout said. "You're welcome to come along."

"Come on, give me a hand with this, Trout, it's worth a fortune."

"You want *all* the lights off?" Annabel asked from a gallery room at the end of the hall.

"Yeah," Trout answered.

"Damn it," Finch said, "you people are costing me a valet for life."

"Let's go," Trout said. He and Roebuck and Annabel walked outside.

"You want me to put him in the back?" Roebuck asked.

Finch made an impressive final attempt to get the rug outside and near the truck. He shoved the boards with all his might and scooted the rug all the way to the front door, where it got stuck because the boards were four or five feet too wide to go through.

"Last call," Trout said, slamming one of the back doors on the truck shut.

"Damn it," Finch said, standing up. He put a foot on a board and ripped it free from the rug. He held the board over his shoulder like a baseball bat and took a couple of steps toward Trout. "If we get two million apiece out of this, it's going to be a *miracle*."

208

Roebuck stepped in front of Finch.

Trout closed the other door and locked the truck.

"Things haven't gone right in so long, we've forgotten how to act," Annabel said.

"Say that again," Trout said to Finch, who still had the board drawn back.

"We'll be lucky to get two million apiece."

The three of them stared unblinkingly at Finch.

He put his board down. After his estimate of their net worth sank in, he shrugged and smiled a little.

Seven

Finch drove the truck with millions of dollars' worth of artwork in the back.

Roebuck rode in the passenger seat and played with the radio.

Trout and Annabel followed along in one of the police cars. Trout said he felt numb. Annabel said she felt ninety.

Finch got the van halfway down the hill. There, he waved his arm out the window and motioned for Trout to pull over.

"I wonder what that's all about?" Trout said.

Annabel looked out her window to the right and guessed there was a bird feeder somewhere that Finch wanted to steal before they left the museum grounds.

Trout stopped his police car, and he and Annabel went forward to see what Finch was so concerned about.

"Quiet," Finch said. "Listen."

"You're not going to believe this," Roebuck said, turning the radio up.

The chief of police was saying:

". . . so we are extremely proud of our people here at the Thirty-third Precinct."

"That's us," Finch said. He opened his door so Trout could stick his head inside and hear better.

Grosvenor kept talking.

"Our officers were held captive by more than a dozen extremely dangerous hoodlums before they escaped by jumping from a third-story warehouse window."

A reporter on the radio asked, "Were you concerned that your refusal to negotiate the ransom could have placed your officers' lives in danger?"

"This particular example of heroism was simply more graphic than most," the chief of police answered. "Our people put their lives on the line every day. This city will not be blackmailed and I believe we have proved that."

The reporter said they would have more with the chief of police, live, in a minute.

Roebuck turned the radio down a little.

Finch was the first to speak. He said, "Why, those damn liars."

What Roebuck wanted to know was how the police from the Thirty-third Precinct had got to be heroes.

"They obviously made up some story to save their rears," Annabel said. "They must feel pretty safe. They must not have thought we got away with anything."

"I don't see why they would have thought *that*," Trout said.

Finch wanted to be sure they all knew what this meant. They all sort of knew but didn't want to press their luck by discussing it.

"It means," Finch said, "they're not coming after us. They're over there taking bows."

"They're not coming after us at the moment, anyway," Trout agreed.

"It means we're the hell home free." Finch fastened his seat belt.

"Don't forget about the toll road on the way to Connecticut," Roebuck told him.

"Oh, hell," Trout said. "We're going to have to rob a gas station for the toll money."

"Here." Annabel took a twenty-dollar bill out of her shoe.

"What was the purpose of *that?*" Trout asked.

"I was saving it for an emergency."

"Like what?"

"A cab home."

"Let's go." Trout closed Finch's door. He was going to follow along in the squad car until they got out of town so nobody would try anything with the truck.

He and Annabel returned to the police car.

They looked up the hill at the museum one last time.

"It really happened," Annabel said, reading Trout's mind.

They turned right at the gate and drove four or five blocks to a small grocery store that was open all night. Trout saw somebody behind the counter and swung past Finch's truck, leading him around the block.

They parked in front of the store.

Trout went inside and picked up two six packs of the best beer in the place.

"What's going on out there?" the man behind the counter asked. He looked from Trout to the police car parked at the curb.

"Nothing."

"Where's your uniform?"

"Oh, Jesus." Trout put the beer on the counter and walked outside. He nodded for Finch to join him at the police car.

Roebuck leaned out the window of his truck.

"He wants to know where my uniform is."

The man inside the store was now at the front window with his nose pressed against the glass.

"And I couldn't think of a thing to say."

"That happened to us at the hospital," Roebuck said. "We went blank."

"You're working undercover," Finch said.

"In a police car?" Trout wondered. He waved at the man in the store. The man in the store nodded slightly.

"Your uniform got ripped off in a fight," Annabel said, yawning.

"How about this," Trout said, rubbing his eyes. "We're making a movie."

Everybody thought that was okay, so Trout tried it on the man in the store who asked, "What'd you go outside for?"

"To get some money."

"What's the name of the movie?"

"It hasn't got one yet," Trout said. "It's one of those quickie porno pictures."

"Don't put my store in it.''

Trout paid for the beer and went outside, where he told Finch to follow him around the corner.

"I'd feel much better about getting drunk in Connecticut," Annabel said.

Trout told her nobody was getting drunk.

They drove around the corner and parked in a lot next to a church, which almost made Finch nervous; but he was thirstier and happier than he was concerned.

They turned off the lights and killed the engines.

Trout took out four beers and put them on the hood of the police car. Each person took a can.

"I'd like to propose a toast," Trout said. "This doesn't mean it's over. We've still got to get to Connecticut without hitting anything. But I think we deserve a break."

The others opened their beers and raised the cans.

"Here's to the arts," Trout said.

"The art of self-defense," Roebuck said.

"And the art of living right," Finch said.

The celebration lasted a mile and a half.

Back in the truck, Finch and Roebuck shook their beer cans and shot foam at each other.

Finch tried to pour some beer on Roebuck's head, but Roebuck was ready. He leaned his head back and drank most of what Finch poured.

Roebuck guessed he felt a little dizzy after only three cans of beer because he hadn't eaten lately.

Finch wanted to buy something. Two blocks from the church parking lot, he tried to buy a garbage truck that was waiting at a red light. Finch offered the driver of the garbage truck eighty thousand dollars but was turned down.

The celebration ended when the beer ran out.

That happened on a one-way street between some brownstones.

Finch and Roebuck ran out of beer first. Finch hit the air horn on his truck and pulled into the left-hand lane. Trout turned on his siren and pulled alongside.

All of this was very loud.

They drove next to each other, going only five miles an hour.

When Roebuck asked for more beer, Trout got a fresh can, popped the tab, leaned out his window, and fizzed it all over the place. Roebuck laughed and ducked. Finch hit the brakes, and most of the foam Trout shot at Roebuck hit the truck's front window.

They made the next green light together, side by side, and Trout tossed Roebuck the last unopened can of beer over a distance of no more than three feet.

Roebuck leaned halfway out his window and made a nice catch.

Trout waved and let the truck pull in front again.

While Trout concentrated on the business at hand, which was driving safely, Annabel stretched out on the front seat. She put her head in Trout's lap and told him how tired and hungry she was. She wondered if they could stop for some food once they were out of town.

"Some *cooked* food," Annabel said. Although they had put some eggs in the icebox in the house in Connecticut, Annabel said she was too tired to strike a match. She was too exhausted even to shower. She was going to jump into the small pond that was out back. She wondered if they might enjoy living in the country somewhere down the line.

"Yeah, I'd love it," Trout said, sipping some beer. "Except for the mosquitoes and snakes and broken pipes and—"

Annabel reached up and held Trout's lips shut.

He bit her finger gently and smiled at Moody's Pharmacy. Moody's Pharmacy was on a corner to Trout's left, and he always grinned when he passed it because *Moody* and *Pharmacy* looked funny together on a sign. There was a cigar-store Indian in the front window of Moody's. Trout always said the Indian had been Moody's first customer, back when the pharmacist was still learning how to mix things.

After Trout smiled at the wooden Indian, he looked to his right and saw the same old book store and, next to it, the bank that had a large set of scales by the front window so, Trout had joked, the customers would see how overweight they were. That would cause them to leave their money in the bank and not spend it on food.

Trout was very familiar with this neighborhood.

He had seen it many times as he and Finch had made the

rounds, determining which streets were wide and which held the least amount of traffic at various times.

Trout had *cased* this damn neighborhood!

As he approached, arrived at, and passed the reducing salon whose window displayed photographs of women weighing seventy-five pounds, he swung his police car left and stuck his head outside. He looked around Finch's truck and down the next block, which was a lot brighter than he had remembered.

Annabel wanted to know what Trout was doing.

Trout sat back behind the wheel and thought about hitting the lights or the siren or even the back of Finch's truck. But it was too late for any of that. Finch was across the intersection.

It was too late for anything except a hard right turn, which Trout made while saying "Oh, Christ."

Finch turned on the windshield wipers and drove by the Thirty-third Precinct.

When Finch turned the windshield wipers on a couple of blocks away from the police station, he succeeded only in smearing around the beer Trout had fizzed at them. Finch left the wipers on and looked through a clear place on Roebuck's side of the windshield. He found and pushed the button that sprayed water from the wiper blades onto the windshield.

He steered with his left hand and held the water button down with his right until the fuzzy figures up ahead and to his left became clearly identifiable as television cameramen, reporters, and police officers.

The majority of these people were on the sidewalk.

Several sat on the steps.

Finch and Roebuck didn't know where they were until they were right on top of the precinct.

"Oh, no," Roebuck said.

He turned off the windshield wipers.

Finch froze. His arms actually became rigid and the truck moved slightly left toward one of the officers who was being interviewed on the sidewalk by a reporter.

For a couple of seconds it appeared that Finch was trying to run over the officer.

Roebuck grabbed the steering wheel and turned it back right.

The first policeman they passed within about ten yards of was Sergeant House, who was telling a reporter what it felt like to swim half a mile in a polluted river. When Sergeant House saw the truck and the two familiar people in it, he ducked and stumbled into the reporter, who dropped his microphone.

"My God, we're back at the precinct," Finch said, his arms still stiff.

"Watch the road," Roebuck said. "Get us out of here." He tried to pry Finch's fingers from around the steering wheel.

The officers out front were every bit as surprised as the two men inside the truck. The only policeman to move— Sergeant House had fallen—was Buck, who was being interviewed just inside the lobby. Buck stepped through the shattered doors and ran down the steps.

"Stop," Lieutenant Bush said to Buck.

The lieutenant was also surprised, but he thought he might know what was happening. He was positive about one thing. His people couldn't just run after a truck that was apparently minding its own business.

"What's going on here?" Grosvenor asked Lieutenant Bush as Buck leaped from the steps to the sidewalk.

It was a fair question.

Sergeant House was on his back.

217

Billows was crouched behind the fender of a station wagon with his arms over his head.

Mounds had run *up* the stairs and was hiding inside the building.

"I'm not certain," Lieutenant Bush told Grosvenor. "But I'll find out."

"Please do. We need to give some more interviews."

Buck turned right and ran *away* from the truck, which was now a few yards past the front doors. Finch's face remained visible, pressed against his window. He watched Buck. He thought Buck was going to run after them, not away. That they hadn't been shot at or even chased loosened Finch up a bit, and he took the wheel back from Roebuck, who wondered again what they were doing *here*.

"Damned if I know," Finch said, looking ahead and then back at the police station, where most of the officers stood with their hands on their hips. "Hang on." Finch stepped on the gas and made a sharp right turn.

Grosvenor again demanded an explanation.

"That truck just turned the wrong way on a one-way street," Lieutenant Bush said. "Also, it might be stolen. Excuse me."

He and a few other officers followed Buck around the building to where the squad cars were parked.

"These people are very dedicated to their jobs," Grosvenor told a reporter standing nearby.

Lieutenant Bush told everybody to remain calm, particularly Buck, who was the first to reach the squad cars. Buck was already in a car when the others arrived and would have driven off had Lieutenant Bush not stepped in front of it.

Buck got out.

"We can't overreact," Lieutenant Bush told the four or

five officers who had run around the building. "We can't draw attention to ourselves, we can't make all that big a deal out of chasing the truck, because we might not catch it."

"That's because we're still standing here," Buck said.

Lieutenant Bush told his officers what he had thought when he saw the truck rolling toward them:

"That they had come back to start again."

"To *what?*" Mounds asked.

"They were going to take us and start again."

"Possible," Sergeant House said. "But that means they haven't gotten away with anything. Let's go home."

"They had no idea we'd make up a story and call a press conference," Lieutenant Bush said.

"That stinks," Buck told him. "They wouldn't start again this close to daylight."

Lieutenant Bush asked Officer Buck for another reason why the truck would return.

"Maybe they were lost," Buck guessed.

Lieutenant Bush said it didn't matter why the truck had returned. There was still one very good reason why it should be pursued, stopped, and searched: "We need to find out if there is anything in the back. We need to find out if they stole anything."

"I'm telling you," Sergeant House said. "If we catch these people, we're through. There's not fifteen of them, heavily armed. There's three or four clowns."

"House," Mounds said, standing beside Buck, "you need to be a little more flexible about this. If there's stolen merchandise in the back of the truck, we need to at least get it. We can return it anonymously."

Sergeant House reminded everybody that even if the people in the truck had stolen something, it didn't matter. "We were kidnapped at the time, remember?"

"It's a matter of pride," Buck said quietly. He got back behind the wheel of his squad car. "They broke the law. They made fools of us."

"I tend to agree," Mounds said, walking to another of the police cars.

"Let's find them and see what's in the back and take it from there," Lieutenant Bush said.

Sergeant House shook his head and said that all they needed was some cheerleaders. "Some *more* cheerleaders."

Mounds pulled the hem of his smock down.

Three police cars sped out of the lot behind the Thirty-third Precinct.

Trout sat at an intersection and looked left and right.

Annabel hit the dashboard and asked, "What the *hell* did he do that for?"

Trout moved through the intersection. He said that Finch's swing by the police station was obviously an accident. "We can't quit now. We've got to see this through."

"An *accident.*"

"We never practiced driving to Connecticut. I mean, from the museum. Remember that one time we all went there? We left from my place."

"*Practiced driving?* All you have to do to get to Connecticut is go to the damn ocean and make a left."

Trout slowed down as he approached another intersection.

"What we should have practiced was drinking beer. Those two drank three sips and went completely out of their minds."

Trout stopped at a corner.

He looked left.

Annabel looked right.

"*There,*" she said.

Finch's truck roared through the intersection a block to the right. It was going the same way Trout was pointed.

Trout stomped the gas pedal and caught up with the truck

at the next intersection. Trout's police car and Finch's truck passed through the green lights, still heading in the same direction, a block away from each other. They were going about forty-five miles an hour.

"It doesn't look like anybody is right behind him," Trout said. "I'll make a right at the next light and cut him off."

"You're on your own," Annabel said. "I quit."

Finch had seen the police car to his left, so he stopped in the middle of the block and somehow backed the van to the intersection he had just passed through.

Roebuck leaned out his window and helped with the backing by giving directions.

He said, "Right, right, left, left," as Finch backed the truck twenty feet. "Left, left, left, right, left."

There were cars parked on both sides of the street, and in the space of about seventy-five yards Finch nearly side-swiped a dozen vehicles, three to his left and eight or nine to his right.

The back of the large van weaved wildly from one side of the street to another.

Finch backed through the intersection and made a left onto a one-way street that, surprisingly enough, ran in the right direction. Finch hit a couple of green lights, made another left onto a very narrow side street, pulled up in front of a cheap hotel, and said, "We lost them, by God."

Roebuck looked around and said that wasn't necessarily good news. "It could have been Trout."

Trout stopped at the intersection a block to his right where Finch should have been.

He got out and looked around.

Annabel refused to look anywhere. She folded her arms and tried to salvage a little something. There was no doubt that all they might get away with now was the squad car in which they sat. Annabel wanted to take the car to New Jersey and sell it. The tires seemed okay. The radio worked. They might be able to get as much as a couple of hundred dollars from a junkyard.

"You let the worst driver in the world lose you. He was in a freight train."

"It's not over," Trout said. "All we have to do is listen for sirens or gunfire."

Finch and Roebuck were also listening for sirens.

Roebuck leaned outside and said, "I hear one. It's to our right."

Finch put the truck in first gear and rolled it a few feet.

"No, wait, Finch. It's *behind* us. It's the lousy echo off the buildings. It might be two sirens, one to the right and one behind."

At least one siren was getting a lot louder.

Roebuck sat back in his seat and said, "They're like bees."

Finch didn't dare expose the truck at another intersection, so he crept past an apartment building and made a left turn into what he hoped might be an alley but turned out to be a loading area. The driveway stopped at an overhead door about fifty or sixty yards from the street.

Finch turned off the lights and the ignition.

He and Roebuck got out of the truck and faced the side street they had just left.

"They find us or they don't," Finch said.

"Then they kill us or they don't," Roebuck added.

Their backs were against the overhead door. There were walls on both sides of them. There was no place to run.

"Can I ask you one question?"

"Sure," Finch said.

"Why'd you drive by the precinct?"

"Beats me. Habit, I guess. Hell, Roebuck, I couldn't see either."

They stood quietly as a police car went by moving right to left. The police car didn't have its siren on. It had its flashing lights on. There were no streetlights mid-block up there, and the vehicle was a blur.

After a few uncomfortable seconds two more police cars flew by, moving in the same directions as the first.

"Maybe we lost them," Roebuck whispered.

This wishful thinking lasted half a minute, tops.

One of the police cars reappeared. It was backing left to right. It was backing slowly. It stopped at the entrance to the driveway, then continued on out of sight.

"Maybe it's Trout," Roebuck whispered.

The other two police cars backed into view, one after the other.

"Maybe they haven't seen us yet," Roebuck said.

The last police car to back into view didn't move on out of sight. It stopped at the driveway and pulled in forward and parked there. The bright lights were turned on, and Finch and Roebuck stood quietly in the headlights.

"I'm all out of maybes," Roebuck said.

The headlights were so bright, Finch couldn't tell how many police officers were running at them. Somebody had a spotlight or flashlight on them too. Judging from the footsteps, it sounded like four or five officers, six at most.

"This is our first offense," Finch yelled at the lights.

Trout wondered for the first time if they really were going to be millionaires.

He sat a block away from the three police cars that were parked by the driveway next to the apartment building.

It was dark up there.

It was also quiet.

"I don't see the truck," Trout said. "I don't see the truck or any ambulances or anything like that."

"I know exactly how you feel," Annabel said. "You can't leave."

"Well, we *could*."

"You could never live with yourself."

"After a while I could."

"You think it might be all right up there. You think the police officers from those cars are checking out something else, or that Finch has captured ten or twelve of them. You can't give up."

"A person has to be practical," Trout said. "You have to have an open mind."

Annabel scooted next to Trout and said that if all this had been her idea, she would undoubtedly feel obligated to ride it right into the ground too. But she was only a foot soldier. She didn't want to be cut down near her prime. She had been in her prime when all this began; now she was just past her prime. "Do what you have to," she said, kissing Trout on the cheek. "I'm going to wait on the corner."

Trout said he at least had to make a gesture. He didn't necessarily have to stop up there by the three police cars. He could drive by or something like that.

Annabel got out and leaned against a parking meter.

Trout drove halfway to the three police cars and stopped.

The squad cars were empty, all right.

And it was unbelievably quiet in all directions.

This made no sense. Somebody should have been walking around or coughing or screaming or *something*. Because this made no sense, Trout started to feel at home again. He looked back at Annabel, who was peeking around the corner. He waved and then inched the car up until he could see part of the way down the driveway, which was as dark as ever.

Trout had two choices.

He could get out and charge into the darkness with his

pistol drawn, or he could go back and get Annabel and go shoplift some breakfast.

Trout had almost decided to head back to the museum and put what he could in the trunk of his police car and make a run for Canada when somebody yelled out of the darkness:

"Hey."

That beat getting shot at, so Trout sat where he was.

"Hey, Trout, is that you?"

Trout scooted across the seat and rolled down the passenger window. He thought about what if anything he should say. After a minute he decided on:

"Yeah, who's that?"

"It's me, Finch. Come on down. We got 'em by the butt."

Six policemen sat in the driveway with their backs against the overhead door and their hands on their heads.

Trout shined his flashlight on each officer, and then on Finch, who waved, and finally on Roebuck, who was sitting calmly on the back bumper of the truck. Trout shined the light back on the police and wondered if this could be some sort of trap.

It certainly didn't look like a trap.

"What's going on here?"

"A cookout," Finch said.

Trout shined his flashlight on everybody concerned one more time before he walked the rest of the way to the truck, where he was hugged by Finch, who said:

"They had no guns."

Finch stepped back and grinned.

"You should have seen it," Roebuck said. "We were scared to death."

"We were moderately concerned," Finch said.

"He about hyperventilated," Roebuck said.

Roebuck shook Trout's hand and said it was great to see him again.

Trout kept blinking.

"Remember when we took their guns, back when all this started," Finch said.

"Two years ago," Roebuck said.

"Back at the police station?"

Trout nodded.

"Back when we put the guns in the lockers across from the ready room? Well, they never got any new guns. So I guess driving by the way I did was actually the smartest thing we could have done."

"What happened," Roebuck said, glancing back at the three police cars parked on the street, "was that they came running up the alley here, yelling for us to surrender. So naturally me and Finch put our hands up."

Finch stood in front of Buck. "This one tried to keep us covered with a key chain."

Finch touched his toe to one of Buck's shoes. "Isn't that the way it happened, Buck?"

Buck didn't move or speak.

"So anyway," Roebuck continued. "It was really pretty simple. It's a good thing they told us to put our hands up instead of throw our guns down. They ran up and stopped and we pointed our guns at them."

"Give us a break," Lieutenant Bush said without looking up.

While Finch kept the police quiet, Trout and Roebuck got the two other squad cars from the street and drove them down the driveway. They opened both trunks and told Lieutenant Bush to make himself comfortable by one of the spares.

"This is beneath contempt," Lieutenant Bush said.

Sergeant House wanted to be left with his dignity.

"What do you need with your dignity?" Finch wondered. "You're heroes. You were kidnapped by terrorists, remember?"

"I'm not sure if we'll get you for this or not," Buck said, stepping into one of the trunks.

Trout told Lieutenant Bush not to worry about suffocating or missing breakfast. Some thieves would undoubtedly break into the cars within the hour.

"Wait," Lieutenant Bush said, propping the trunk open with a foot. "Tell me one thing. Have you stolen anything?"

"No, not yet," Trout said.

They locked the police in the trunks and got into the truck and picked up Annabel at the corner. They were almost out of town by the time Finch finished telling her about their close call.

It took him fifteen minutes to explain how the police had done fifteen seconds worth of running.

Annabel found it all very interesting but said that if anybody started celebrating again, she'd shoot him.

They were in a much better mood when they stopped at a coffee shop on the turnpike to get some food.

It was a relief to be out of the city.

About all they had to avoid now was traffic.

Trout and Roebuck stayed with the truck while Finch and Annabel went inside, where they were waited on by a woman who was wearing four or five coats of lipstick.

Finch went to the men's room first and reported back to the waitress that it needed raking.

"I guess this means you're going to take your seal back," the waitress said.

"Seal?"

"You're not with *Good Housekeeping?*"

"We're with the Health Department," Finch said. "We heard you haven't got all the bugs worked out of your kitchen."

"We got *most* of them," the waitress said.

"Knock it off," Annabel said.

Finch whispered to her that he was only acting natural; Annabel needed to loosen up, or else she would attract attention.

Finch then asked about some food.

The waitress said they had all kinds at all hours, even seafood.

"Like what?" Finch wondered.

"Saltwater taffy," the waitress answered. "And shrimp omelettes."

Annabel ordered ten dollars' worth of eggs and bacon and orange juice and coffee.

"That's one order," the waitress said. She told Finch he ought to stop in more often. He wasn't bad looking for this time of the morning.

"For the love of God," Annabel said. "Get us the food."

"Your wife?" the waitress asked Finch.

"Aunt."

While Finch and Annabel waited for the food, Trout and Roebuck had an attendant check the left rear tire, which was the spare they had put on after Finch had flattened the original.

Roebuck unlocked the back doors and peeked inside to check on the artwork. He told Trout everything was fine.

"What'd you expect?"

"There's no telling," Roebuck said.

Trout went to see what was going on with the food.

"What are you hauling?" the attendant asked.

"Parts," Roebuck said.

"Where you headed?"

"Maine."

"Which town you headed for?"

"A little one."

"What kind of parts?"

"What is this crap?" Roebuck said.

The attendant pardoned the hell out of himself.

Roebuck closed the back doors on the truck and helped

228

Annabel with some of the food. He held it at arm's length so the grease wouldn't eat a hole in his shirt.

Finch drove. Roebuck sat in the middle. Annabel sat on Trout's lap by the window.

The waitress stepped outside and told Finch to be sure and come back.

"He knocked her off her feet," Annabel said.

Roebuck leaned up for a look at the waitress and said it didn't look like this was the first time she had been knocked down.

Finch honked good-bye and maneuvered the rig back onto the turnpike, carefully avoiding several signs on the re-entry ramp.

Quackenbush was the luckiest person in the world.

He was suspended four or five feet over a dirt road that contained some very deep and jagged ruts. He was moving. It had happened so suddenly, the only thing Quackenbush could think of that might save his life was to kick his feet. But that didn't work. It only made him tired and weakened his grip. So he quit kicking and simply hung there with his hands tightly wrapped around the inside-door handle.

But at least he was a free man.

Quackenbush could see the dirt road in the glow from the taillights. He estimated that he was traveling forty or forty-five miles an hour and wondered what would happen if he let go of the handle.

His feet would hit first, and one of them would probably break. His head would hit next and that would probably break too. His feet and head would keep hitting the dirt road for about a block, and then it would be up to somebody else to say what would happen next—the paramedic, if they had one out here.

Quackenbush had no choice except to hang on.

He hung there until the truck made a sharp right turn, which propelled the door from which Quackenbush dangled back shut. The door swung shut very quickly and forcefully, and Quackenbush was thrown into the middle of the truck.

He landed on some artwork wrapped with thick blankets and decided that this overtime was going to look very impressive on his resumé.

Quackenbush hadn't known what to think for quite a while, beginning with when they locked him in the back of the truck with the masterpieces.

That had happened during the argument when the shorter man about hit the taller man with a board. Quackenbush had been toward the front of the van wrapping a large Giordano when the doors were slammed shut.

He had been hidden by some other large paintings.

Quackenbush naturally thought they had shut him inside on purpose because, after all, he couldn't get out. He had tried the doors a number of times, and in each instance they had been locked from the outside.

So what Quackenbush had concluded shortly after they had locked him in was that they would need some help with the unwrapping or storage of the artwork; that, or they would need some help negotiating with the board of directors. Quackenbush wondered if he had been brought along so he could tell the board that the artwork had not been damaged.

Maybe they expected him to drive the artwork back to the museum.

Quackenbush changed his mind the last time he checked the doors.

That was shortly after Roebuck had peeked inside. Quackenbush had hidden behind the Giordano and wondered why nobody said anything. He had stayed hidden and waited until the truck had been moving awhile before checking the doors again. As he pushed the handle down, the truck made a quick turn, and that was why Quackenbush had almost flown out.

He hadn't expected the doors to be open.

Quackenbush got off the blankets he had been thrown onto. He walked to the right-hand door and opened it. He threw a painting out. He spread his feet for balance, held the door open with his right hand, and sailed the small painting into a ditch as the truck was rolling slowly through a left turn.

The painting was light, and it flew into some weeds and landed without a sound.

Quackenbush didn't throw anything else outside until the truck made another slow left turn. He did his best work on one turn that was so severe the van almost stopped. He threw out nine paintings, all securely wrapped in blankets, during that one sweeping curve, and five or six more on a similar hairpin a few seconds later.

Quackenbush worked quietly, but it didn't matter. Annabel was asleep. Roebuck was about to be. Finch was concentrating on what road there was. Trout was looking at the inventory list, trying to determine exactly how many millions of dollars' worth of artwork they had in the back.

He guessed twenty-two million.

The radio was on.

As Quackenbush established a rhythm, he managed to relocate the majority of the paintings and precious works of art in the space of what he guessed to be a mile or so. He had a miserable time with the large Giordano. He couldn't sail it. It was too heavy. He had to roll it out. He heaved the Giordano with all his might. The hell with the frame. Let it crack. The Giordano hit the edge of the dirt road with one of its points and kicked a couple of feet into the air before settling snugly into a ditch, which Quackenbush guessed was three feet deep.

Quackenbush could have thrown everything out.

He had the bust of Alexander the Great all the way to the door and was ready to pitch it. It was a beautifully preserved bust. The board of directors was extremely fond of Alexander the Great. Quackenbush could have tossed it out easy as you please.

But he just didn't.

He would tell the board of directors that the people in the truck had carried the bust and a couple of other items up front in the cab. He couldn't tell the board that he simply hadn't felt like throwing Alexander the Great into the weeds.

But he gave it a lot of thought.

And that was the way he felt.

And that was all there was to it.

Quackenbush had no idea what those poor people up front deserved.

But he knew what he deserved: He deserved to have been locked in a closet.

So he put the bust on a blanket in the middle of the truck with a note:

Don't drop this.

Quackenbush was at his most heroic when he jumped out of the van. He put two oriental vases wrapped in blankets under his left arm, and a bust of a Greek commoner under his right arm, and he jumped sideways out of the van during another of those handy slow left turns. The truck wasn't going much more than ten miles an hour. Still, Quackenbush almost broke both legs and his neck, and then he almost drowned.

He landed at the edge of the dirt road. His feet flew out from under him, and he did a half-cartwheel with his head leading the way toward the ditch, which emptied into a creek. He slid down the bank on his back, holding the vases away from his stomach, and came to rest in six inches of muddy water.

The truck straightened out after the turn and the rear door swung shut.

Quackenbush was at peace with himself as he limped through the weeds collecting art.

He picked things up from beside the dirt road and relocated them near a line of trees about fifty yards from the ditch.

There were people in this world who would give anything to have breakfast with Alexander the Great.

Quackenbush smiled at the prospect of that. Surely the people in the truck could take it from there. They wouldn't drive off a bridge, would they?

The large Giordano had come to rest beside a driveway that led to a cabin set back in some tall pines. Quackenbush lugged the Giordano to the cabin and pounded on the front door until a man wearing a robe answered. Quackenbush told the man a story about having trouble with his truck and offered a five-hundred-dollar reward for some help with the things that had fallen out of the back.

The man woke his wife, who seemed a bit suspicious at first. But eventually they agreed to lend a hand. The woman made a fresh pot of coffee and put it in a Thermos. Then the three of them got in a pickup truck and began collecting the artwork.

Eight

Had they gotten away with the two or so million apiece, Trout said, they would have gotten stale.

Maybe all this meant was that there was *four* million apiece waiting for them somewhere down the road.

They had their health.

You couldn't put a price tag on that.

Trout said you couldn't buy happiness.

"Quack," the duck said.

"You're right," Trout said as the duck paddled away. "We could have *rented* a hell of a lot of happiness."

He quit rehearsing a speech.

He put Alexander the Great on the front porch with Quackenbush's note and went for a walk. He walked about a quarter of a mile from the rented house in the Connecticut countryside and watched the sunrise from a knoll.

This beats looking at the world through the peephole of

an apartment door, Trout thought as the sky turned salmon-colored.

They sat at the kitchen table—the bust of Alexander the Great was the centerpiece—trying to think of somebody to blame.

Strangely enough, nobody was bitching.

This condition—where you sat quietly and stared at the walls—was called shock, Finch said.

A washcloth was wrapped around the knuckles on his right hand. He had slugged a wall. "You could have prepared us," Finch said.

Trout told them that nobody had prepared him: While they were inside the rented house eating, he had opened the back doors on the truck, and there the damn head was, staring at him.

It was a miracle he hadn't fainted.

They sighed.

They could have locked the doors after they checked on the art at the restaurant on the turnpike.

They could have shot the guards.

And, of course, they could have gotten away with nothing except a rosy glow on their cheeks.

"Don't push this health crap too far," Finch said.

"If a pig had wings," Roebuck said.

Annabel wanted to know what that was supposed to mean.

Roebuck had no idea.

At least, they seemed to agree tacitly, it was *over*.

Morning had come. The skies had cleared and the kitchen in the rented house was yellow with sunshine.

Trout's left eye was nearly puffed shut. Something had bitten him at sunrise—a black widow spider, Finch guessed.

They drank some coffee and wondered what they were supposed to do now. Trout decided to try the museum. Maybe the telephone lines had been repaired.

"Don't talk so long they can trace the call," Roebuck said.

Trout nodded his thanks for that suggestion; God love them, they were still in there swinging.

Trout's call to the museum was answered after two rings.

"We've got some of your stuff here," he said.

"Yes, yes, we're aware of that," the person on the other end said.

"Who are you?"

"My name is Granger. I'm the chairman of the board. Several other members are here and we're prepared to get on with this."

"Where's Quackenbush?" Trout didn't know whether to thank or threaten the guard.

"Resting comfortably."

"We've got these damn racks," Trout said, picking one up off the floor. They had been in a corner of the van, under some blankets.

"Don't make it sound like they're *rotten*," Annabel said.

"We've got these great damn racks."

"They're French fire dogs," Granger said. "They hold logs, firewood."

"How much?"

"The set is worth thirty-three hundred dollars. I have been authorized to offer eleven hundred dollars for both pieces, which is more than fair."

Trout looked at one of the French fire-dog-log-holders and tended to agree. He wrote the eleven-hundred-dollar figure on a piece of paper and passed it around.

"You murdered them on that one," Finch said.

"Okay, what about the head?" Trout said into the phone. Granger didn't answer.

"You try to cheat us, I'll smash it into chalk."

"I'll be frank. It's extremely valuable. We will pay twenty thousand dollars for its safe return."

"What's it worth?" Trout asked.

"It's debatable."

"We could try to sell it to a collector."

"We'd be forced to inform the authorities."

"Sold." Trout wrote twenty thousand dollars on the paper underneath the eleven hundred for the French fire dogs.

"Shall I mail you a check?" Granger asked.

Trout told him he wasn't dealing with amateurs; they had an account in Switzerland, and everything.

"Fine, fine."

"Hold it right there," Finch said.

He stood up and leaned across the table and took the telephone. "All right, pal," he said to Granger. "What'd you *really* offer for this head?"

"I told you, twenty thousand."

"Sorry," Finch said, handing the telephone back to Trout. "I thought you were trying to put one over on us."

Trout told the chairman of the board they'd take the twenty-one thousand one hundred dollars. He said he'd call back later with the bank account number and the address where Alexander the Great and the racks could be picked up.

He hung up and divided what they had coming by four.

"Not bad for a lifetime's work," Annabel said.

Trout turned the piece of paper over and drew something.

"What do you think about this?" he asked, pushing his sketch into the middle of the table so everybody could see.

"What is it?" Finch wondered.

"It looks like an outhouse," Roebuck said.

"It's a bank," Trout said. "In a way. It's one of those tiny banks."

Annabel got up and went to bed.

Epilogue

SERGEANT HOUSE organized the desk officers around town, and they demanded safer working conditions. They demanded bullet-proof cubicles. Two weeks after Sergeant House's cubicle was up, a thief locked him inside and stole some furniture.

MOUNDS traded in his Lincoln for a used Rolls. A newspaper reporter writing a series about questionable behavior within the police department pointed out that Mounds made twenty-nine thousand dollars a year but drove a car worth three times that much. Mounds demanded and received a front-page correction that cleared up any suggestion of wrongdoing. The correction said that Officer Mounds lived at the YMCA.

LIEUTENANT BUSH was promoted. At least the department said it was a promotion, but Bush knew he was being punished for threatening the silly damn strike. During Bush's first week as captain of the dreaded Eighty-seventh Precinct, somebody threw a brick through his office window. The second week, one of his beat officers took a swing at him. He's the only police captain in town who uses a private bodyguard when he has to make his occasional rounds.

GROSVENOR AND HIS WIFE are separated. Two weeks before the election, Grosvenor was punched in the mouth by a pimp and wasn't able to make more speeches. He lost by ten thousand votes in the gubernatorial primary.

BUCK replaced Bush as lieutenant of the graveyard shift at the Thirty-third Precinct and, during the first month of his command, helped tow off fifty cars. The small-business men and women of the area got together and made up some serious crimes to take Buck's mind off their cars. The nighttime crime rate went up so much because of the phony crimes that Buck was transferred out of everybody's hair.

LOVELY told the museum he found the antique French commode in an alley. He lost the five-hundred-dollar reward playing poker.

PIKE AND SUGGS kidnapped a sheriff and two deputies in a small town in Arizona so their entry into a jewelry store wouldn't be noticed. They ran the U-Haul truck, with the sheriff and the deputies in the back, into the middle of a funeral procession and were arrested.

ABE GINSBERG tried a photo of Jane Fonda in the window of his bakery. The inscription said: "Dear Abe, these cinnamon rolls are the best things I've ever eaten in my life." That worked so well, he was going to try some photos of other celebrities who lived thousands of miles away.

QUACKENBUSH was the first nonmillionaire elected to the board of directors at the museum.

ANNABEL decided to pass the time until Trout snapped out of it serving as president of Burials at Sea, Inc. She bought

239

an old fishing boat and fixed it up. She hauls poor or middle-class souls into International Waters. Her basic service, which includes oceanic charts showing the burial site, costs two hundred and fifty dollars. A Weekend Special with some deep-sea fishing on the way in is four hundred and fifty dollars.

FINCH has stayed in and out of trouble renting dogs. He rents mutts he picks up at the pound, with options to buy. Except for a part Collie that dragged a kid through a busy intersection, Finch is hanging in there.

ROEBUCK started a professional football predicting service. He missed nine games in a row the second and third weeks of the season and was down to four customers, one of whom worked for the Better Business Bureau. The fourth week of the season, Roebuck hired a fortune-teller who got five games, missed six, and became a partner.

TROUT was slow getting back to work after he received his $5,275 for masterminding the Crime of the Century. He was a little depressed at first and didn't leave his apartment for a week or so. But after his friends stopped by—Finch brought some TV dinners, Annabel brought some pajamas that had *feet*, for God's sake, and Roebuck gave him the Jets over the Dolphins free of charge—he got busy with the idea that in his opinion would make the museum business look like a prank. Trout's plan was to construct a fake cubicle like the ones banks use for after-hours deposits in the suburbs. Once Trout had polished his plan a few times, the four of them would haul this arrangement to a busy shopping center on a Friday night and sit inside over the weekend, collecting cash.

JAY CRONLEY lives in Tulsa, Oklahoma, where he writes a thrice weekly newspaper column for the Tulsa *Tribune*. He is a frequent contributor to *Playboy* magazine and has won two *Playboy* writing awards for nonfiction. *Cheap Shot* is his fifth novel.

DATE			